THE GUNSMITH

463

The Gunsmith Women's Club

THE GUNSMITH

463

The Gunsmith Women's Club

J.R. Roberts

SPEAKING VOLUMES, LLC
NAPLES, FLORIDA
2020

The Gunsmith Women's Club

ISBN 978-1-64540-320-3

Chapter One

Three women sat at a campfire waiting for the coffee, bacon and beans to be ready. Maggie Streeter looked across at Amy Logan and Nell Livingston.

"Nell," she said, "how do you feel?"

"Tired," Nell said. "But I'll be fine."

"You think he's gonna be here?" Amy asked.

Maggie looked at them both. Amy and Nell were in their late twenties, while Maggie was ten years older. For that reason, they were following her.

"That's what I heard," Maggie said. "He was there, and hopefully he's still there."

Amy looked over at the horses and the buggy, which was for Nell, since she wasn't well enough to ride.

"Nell and me, we think you should go on ahead, Maggie," she said. "You'll move faster without us."

"Will you be all right?" Maggie asked.

"We'll keep movin'," Amy said, "it'll just take us a little longer to get there. But maybe you can get there in time to keep him from leavin'."

"You might be right," Maggie said. She looked at the pan on the fire. "The food's ready. Let's eat."

She doled out the bacon-and-beans and they started in on the food.

They were searching for Clint Adams and had been for over a month. All three had history with him, but that didn't mean he was going to remember them if and when they found him. After all, he had been traveling for years, meeting people—women—and leaving them behind. How could he possibly remember everyone he'd dealt with?

Maggie liked to think he'd remember her. They had spent the better part of a week together, eating, drinking and making love. According to Amy, she'd been with him for three days. And Nell said they had been together only a few times, but she was sure he was the one.

When they finished eating, they allowed Nell to bed down underneath the buggy, while the two of them cleaned up.

"Is she gonna make it?" Amy asked. "She's gettin' weaker."

"She needs a doctor," Maggie said.

"She won't take the time to see one until we find him," Amy said.

"Then we better find him soon."

"Do you think he'll remember?" Amy asked.

"I don't know if he will or not," Maggie said, "but he's a decent man. He'll do the right thing, once we explain."

"I hope so," Amy said.

"You spent time with him, Amy," Maggie said. "You know what kind of man he is."

"I know what kind of man he was, back then," Amy said, "but that was years ago."

"He couldn't have changed that much," Maggie said. "Not Clint Adams."

"I wish I was as confident as you are," Amy said, "but I didn't spend as much time with him as you did."

Maggie put her hand on Amy's arm.

"Don't worry," she said, "he'll be the same man we were all with."

"I hope you're right."

"You better turn in," Maggie said.

"You, too."

Maggie nodded. There was no reason for one of them to stay on watch. Nobody was chasing them. They were the ones doing the chasing.

***

Maggie rose first in the morning, got the bacon and coffee going. Nell rolled out from underneath the buggy and came walking over.

"You sleep all right?" Maggie asked.

"Well enough."

Maggie helped Nell sit down by the fire, handed her a cup of steaming hot coffee. It wasn't cold out, but Nell still looked like she was shivering. And there was a sheen of sweat on her forehead. Maggie was sure the woman had a fever.

"Nell," she said, "even if we get to this town and he's not there, you're gonna have to see a doctor."

"I know," Nell said.

"No argument?"

Nell smiled wanly.

"No argument."

"Good girl."

Amy came walking over, and Maggie handed her a cup.

"Nell's agreed to see a doctor when we reach this town," Maggie said.

"Good," Amy said. "Hopefully Clint will be there, and then we can start back."

"If he comes with us," Nell said.

"He will," Maggie said. "Don't worry, he will."

Chapter Two

Clint Adams looked down at the three aces in his hand. He'd managed to bluff a few hands, but for the most part, his luck had been good. This was an example. He'd been dealt three aces, and one of the players in front of him had opened the betting. His options were to call or raise. If he raised, some of the other players might drop out too soon. Just calling might keep everyone and their money in the hand a bit longer. Of course, somebody else might improve their hand, but since his luck had been running, he decided to take the chance.

"I call."

The player who had opened drew one card. Clint asked for two. The other players made their draws, and Clint had the impression they were all trying to improve. He figured he only had to worry about the opener, who probably had two pair.

Clint had played in high stakes as well as penny ante games. This one was somewhere in-between.

"Twenty dollars," the opener said.

The next player folded.

Clint was next.

"Raise," he said, "twenty more."

The next player folded. The fifth player called, but Clint knew it was because he never folded.

The opener, a man named Happ, stared across the table at Clint.

"You've bluffed me twice already, Adams," he said.

"Is that your read on me?" Clint asked.

"That's it," Happ said, with satisfaction. "You might be foolin' these others, but you don't fool me." He counted out some money from what he had left on the table. "Raise a hundred."

That brought a sigh from the other players at the table. It was the largest bet of the day.

Clint thought Happ was putting a lot of faith in two pair and his feeling that Clint was bluffing, again.

"Well," Clint said, "you don't win if you don't try, right? Your hundred, and another two."

Happ glared at him as the other players sighed again—or maybe it was a collective gasp. The Dead Cowboy Saloon was the largest in Big Fork, Arizona, but they had never seen betting like this before.

"You know, if I call that bet, I'm tapped out," Happ went on.

"Are you?" Clint asked. "I'm afraid I haven't been paying that much attention to how much money you have in front of you, Mr. Happ."

"You've been payin' attention to everythin' that happens on this table," Happ said, "but this time you're just tryin' too hard."

Clint knew the man could call the bet, but if he wanted to raise, he'd have to offer a marker or borrow the money.

Happ looked around the room, possibly seeking someone for the loan. Apparently not seeing anyone, he counted out the money in front of him.

"I've got two hundred and fifty here," he said, "so I'll raise fifty. If you raise again, you're gonna have to take my marker."

Clint knew that was one option. The other was for him to raise Happ, not take the man's marker, and force him to drop out. Either way, this would be a lesson for the younger man.

"I tell you what, Mr. Happ," Clint said, "I'll just call your raise." He pushed the money into the pot.

"Ha!" Happ said, slapping his cards down onto the table, face up. "Kings over Jacks."

"Three Aces," Clint said, laying his cards down gently.

"Aces win," the dealer said.

"What the hell—?" Happ's eyes widened. "You weren't bluffin'?"

"Not this time."

Clint raked in his pot.

"Nice playing with you, Mr. Happ," he said. "Whose deal is it?"

One of the other players picked up the cards, shuffled, said, "Five card stud," and started dealing. Happ was still seated, so the deal went around him.

"Hey, wait!" he snapped.

"You have no money on the table, Happ," the dealer said. "You're out."

"I can get more money!" Happ cried.

"Then do that," one of the other players said, "and then come back."

"Are you givin' up that seat?" a man standing by asked. He'd been waiting almost half-an-hour for a seat to open up for him.

"No!" Happ said.

"Yes, he is," Clint said. "Go ahead, Mr. Happ. Take a break."

With all the men watching him—seated and standing—Uriah Happ finally stood up and, eyes glazed, walked away from the table on stiff legs.

"King bets," the dealer said.

Chapter Three

The woman standing at the bar had attracted attention when she entered the saloon.

"You in the right place, lady?" the bartender asked when she appeared.

"You got beer?" she asked.

"I do."

"Then I'm in the right place. I'll have one."

"Comin' up."

She nursed the beer and watched Clint Adams play poker. It had been five years since she'd seen him last. She and her partners had been trying to find him for months. There was a time when they might have found him in Labyrinth, Texas, or left a message for him there, but that time was passed. He didn't go to that town, anymore.

"Hey," she called to the bartender.

"Yeah?"

"How long has he been here in Big Fork?"

"Who?"

"The Gunsmith," she said. "Over there, at the poker table. Come on, you know who he is."

"Yeah, I do," he said. "He's been playin' there a coupla hours."

"Do you know how long he's been in town?" she asked. "How long he's stayin'?"

"He's been here a few days," the bartender said. "He don't seem in a hurry to get outta here, or Arizona."

"Is there a woman?"

"What?"

"Is there a woman he's interested in?"

"I don't know," the bartender said. "I don't pay that close attention to my customers."

"How many customers have you had like the Gunsmith?" she asked.

The bartender hesitated, then said, "He's been seen with a woman named Katie Bowman. She runs a rooming house."

"Is he stayin' there?"

"He is."

"Where is it?"

"South end of town." He stared at her. "Why the hell am I answerin' all your questions?"

The woman shrugged and said, "I guess I have that kind of face."

She turned and walked out of the saloon, sure that Clint Adams hadn't seen her. Once outside, she went looking for the telegraph office.

***

Clint glanced over at the bar, saw that Maggie Streeter had left the saloon. He had seen her enter, was sure she had seen him, but she hadn't approached him. There must have been a reason for that, so he stayed where he was. If she wanted to talk to him, he would see her again.

After Uriah Happ left the table, his place was taken by a man named Tom Lennox. He was a better player than Happ had been. Most of the money on the table had been in front of Clint, but now some of it had made its way across to Lennox. Clint knew if he played long enough, he could get it back, but he really didn't want to spend that much more time at the game. He was getting hungry.

"Deal me out," he said, picking up his money.

"You pullin' out?" Lennox asked.

"For tonight," Clint said. "I'll probably be back tomorrow."

"Good," Lennox said. "I'll look forward to seein' you then."

Clint got up from the table and left the saloon. There was a café across the street that he had been eating at since his arrival three days before. He went there and got a table in the back. While he was eating, Maggie Streeter entered the café. He wasn't surprised because he had spotted her outside.

She walked over to him and smiled.

"Remember me?"

"Of course, Maggie," he said. "Have a seat."

She sat down, looking relieved, removed her hat and ran her hands through her long dark hair.

"It's been a while," he said.

"Years," she said. "Tell me I look older."

"Only more beautiful than ever," he said, instead.

"I was hopin' that you hadn't changed," she said. "That you were still a decent, honorable man."

"I don't know about that," he said, "but I'm still the man you knew."

"We were countin' on that," she said.

A waiter came over and Clint ordered a steak, then told him to bring Maggie whatever she wanted.

"I don't have much money," Maggie said.

"Don't worry about that," Clint said.

"Steak," she said to the waiter.

"Comin' up!"

"We?" Clint said.

"Sorry?"

"You said 'we' were hoping," he said. "Who's we?"

"I have a story to tell you."

Chapter Four

Five years earlier . . .

Clint met Maggie Streeter five years before, in a town called Kindred, Wyoming. He rode in looking for his friend, Bat Masterson, but quickly found out that Bat had never been there. By that time, however, he had laid eyes on Maggie Streeter, a beautiful brunette in her early thirties who, oddly enough, owned and ran a hardware store.

He saw her walking down the street, wearing a blue dress, kept his eyes on her until she went into the hardware store.

"Pretty lady, huh?"

He turned, saw a man wearing a badge looking at him.

"She sure is," Clint said. "Wonder what's she's doing in a hardware store?"

"That's easy," the lawman said. "She owns it."

"A hardware store?"

"It was her husband's," the sheriff said, "but he died a few years back. I'm Sheriff Logan. You're a stranger in town."

"I am," Clint said. "My name's Clint Adams."

The sheriff looked surprised.

"What's the Gunsmith doin' in a town like Kindred?" he asked. "We're small, and there ain't much goin' on here."

"I was looking for a friend of mine," Clint said. "Bat Masterson."

"Well," the sheriff said, "if a man like Bat Masterson had been here, I'd know about it."

"I suppose you would."

"Sorry to disappoint you."

"No problem," Clint said. "I hadn't seen him in a while, and thought I'd catch up."

"So, since he's not here, will you be movin' on?"

"I don't know," Clint said. "I have a sudden urge to buy a hammer."

Sheriff Logan, a man in his forties, gave Clint a knowing look and said, "Well, good luck. There have been quite a few men in this town tryin' to buy that hammer. It might not be so easy."

"Thanks for the warning," Clint said.

"Speakin' of warnin's," the sheriff said, "try not to kill anybody while you're in town, will you?"

"I'll do my best," Clint promised.

The sheriff walked away, and Clint crossed the street to the hardware store.

***

Clint had spent only a short time in the store, before he and Maggie Streeter connected. She not only agreed to have supper with him that night but, to his surprise, went back to his hotel with him.

When they entered the room, she turned to him, quickly coming into his arms, and kissed him feverishly.

"Don't look so surprised," she said. "I've been alone for years, and you're the first man in all that time who's interested me."

"I'm flattered."

"And, as you'll see," she said, unbuttoning his shirt, "you're also lucky."

She undressed him quickly, pulled off his boots, gave him time to hang his gunbelt within easy reach, then sat him on the bed, nude, to watch her undress.

She peeled the dress off slowly, and had obviously planned for this, because she had no undergarments on, at all. She simply shrugged off the dress and stood before him, naked. She was full bodied, with large, well rounded breasts and buttocks, beautifully shaped thighs and legs. She allowed him to take it all in, and by this time, his cock was standing straight and hard, jutting out from his crotch.

"Oh my," she said, falling to her knees in front of him. "I hope you don't mind if this takes a while."

"I'm in no hurry."

She took his hard penis in her hot hands, stroked it, seemed to examine it thoroughly before finally leaning forward and touching her lips to it. She kissed it, licked it, wet it with her tongue, and then finally engulfed it. If he thought her hands were hot, her mouth was steaming.

She sucked him avidly, one hand around the base of his cock and the other fondling his testicles. He leaned back on his hands and watched as her head bobbed up and down on him. She hadn't been kidding about warning him that it would take a while. Several times he felt as if he was going to explode, but she did something with her hands that stopped him, then continued to suck.

"Jesus," he said, the fourth time she stopped him, "where did you learn this?"

"I had a friend who was a prostitute," she answered, looking up at him. "She taught me everything she knew."

"But you were never—"

"—a whore? No," she said, "I just wanted to know what a whore knows."

She stood up then, slid onto his lap and kissed him again, crushing their bodies together so that his cock was trapped between them.

He ran his hands down her bare back, until he reached her butt cheeks, which he held in his palms.

"I know," she said, "I have a big ass."

"You have a great one," he said, squeezing it. "Nice and firm and round. Just the way I like it."

"You like meaty women?" she asked.

She leaned back so he could see her large breasts.

"Oh, yes," he said, staring at her dark nipples, "you can definitely say I like my women . . . meaty."

"Well then," she said, shaking her shoulders and jiggling her breasts, "enjoy."

He bent his head and did.

Chapter Five

The present . . .

"Do you remember Amy Logan?" Maggie Streeter asked Clint.

"Amy . . . yes, I do remember," Clint said. "I met her a few years ago, somewhere in Montana. How do you two know each other?"

"We ran into each other, got to talking, one thing led to another, and we discovered that we both knew you . . . real well."

"Ah . . . and where is she?" he asked, cutting into his steak.

"She's actually on her way here," she said.

"Here? To Big Fork?"

Maggie nodded.

"Remember I told you I had a story to tell you?" Maggie asked. "Amy and me, we've been looking for you for some time."

"Oh yeah? Why?"

"I think I'm going to wait until she gets here to tell you the whole story," Maggie said,

"And when will she be here?" he asked.

"A day or two," Maggie said. "Will you still be in town?"

"I suppose so," he said. "I'm not really in a hurry to get anywhere."

"And you have a friend here, right?"

"A friend?"

"The rooming house lady?"

"Ah, Katie . . ."

"Right, Bowman," Maggie said. "That's what the bartender said."

"I'm just one of her roomers," Clint said.

"Right," Maggie said. "Don't worry. I'm not the jealous type."

"You said you've been looking for me?" Clint asked. "How'd you know I was here, in Big Fork?"

"Word gets around," Maggie said, "especially when you ask."

"I don't think I like the word getting around," Clint said.

"Come on," Maggie said, "you must know by now how people talk when the Gunsmith comes to town."

"I try to keep low," he explained.

"Playing poker?" she asked.

She had a point. Playing poker and winning was not the way to keep your head down. He hadn't been playing as much as he used to. Maybe it was time to stop altogether, if he wanted to keep drifting without word getting around where he was.

"Good point," he told her.

***

After they finished eating, they left the café and stopped out front.

"I'd invite you to my room, Maggie, but you know, it's a rooming house."

"Yes," Maggie said, "and your landlady probably doesn't like women in the rooms."

"You've got that right," he said.

"Well," she said, "*I* have a hotel room."

"Is that an invitation?"

She shrugged and said, "It could be . . ."

***

He remembered her body very well. The curves, the shadows, the sounds she made when he touched her. It had been a while since he'd seen her, and she had put on some weight, but it was all in the right places—places he liked putting his hands, his mouth, his tongue . . .

She moaned, pushed his head away from her crotch and rolled away from him.

"My God, I forgot how good you are at that," she said.

"I'm not finished," he told her.

"Wait, wait . . ." she said, putting her hands out. "Give me a minute. Are you sure your landlady friend won't be looking for you?"

"I told you," Clint said, "I'm just one of her roomers."

"Is that the truth?" she asked. "You're not sleeping with her?"

"No," he said, "I mean, yes it's the truth, and no I'm not sleeping with her. Not that it might not have happened if you hadn't come to town."

"I'm sorry to ruin your plans," she said.

"Maggie," he said, "you're special—"

"Do you say that to all the women you're with?" she asked. "Did you say it to Amy?"

"I probably say it to every woman I'm with, because I'm usually with special women."

Maggie thought about Nell, but decided not to bring her up, yet.

"Oh, all right," she said, putting her arms out to him. "Come and make me feel even more special. I'm not going to argue with you about it."

He smiled and moved into her embrace.

Chapter Six

Clint was telling the truth about Katie Bowman. His landlady was a pleasant, attractive woman in her late thirties, but she was also a fervent church goer. Although they had been seen walking around town together, and dining, they had not shared a bed. Now, with Maggie in town, that would probably be the furthest thing from his mind.

He stayed with Maggie in her room that night, and they had breakfast together.

"Tell me about you and Amy," he said.

"What do you want to know?" she asked.

"What do you have in common?" he asked. "Other than me, that is."

"Not much," she admitted. Other than wanting to help Nell, of course.

"What happened to your hardware store?"

"Oh that," she said. "I had to give it up."

"Why?"

"A large mercantile opened in town, and they were underselling me. I simply . . . went out of business."

"And then what?"

"And then I traveled a bit. Eventually, the traveling became drifting."

"I know about that," Clint said.

"I'm sure you do," she said. "While drifting I ran into Amy."

"And what was she doing?"

"Trying to make her ranch work," Maggie said. "You remember her ranch?"

"I do," he said. "Her husband died, and she tried to make a go of it alone. What happened?"

"After you left, she kept at it for a couple of years, but finally the bank took it. When I got to town, she was working in the saloon."

"That's a shame," he said. "She didn't belong in a saloon."

"That's what I thought, so I invited her to ride with me a while, and she said yes. It was while talking over a campfire that we realized we both knew you."

"And you decided to track me down?"

"There was another reason for that," she said, "but I'm still going wait for Amy to get here before telling you."

"Well, you've got me curious," he said, "so I'll wait around, too."

"It won't be long," she said. "I came ahead because I could move faster alone."

"Is there some reason Amy couldn't keep up with you?" he asked.

She hesitated a moment, then said, "Well, there's a buggy involved."

"Oh, I get it," he said, and didn't ask any further questions.

***

Clint decided since he had already started to play poker, and word had probably already gotten around, that he'd continue to play. In the future, though, he was going to pick and choose carefully when he played and when he didn't.

He told Maggie he'd be in the saloon whenever she wanted to find him. When he got to the Dead Cowboy, the game was going on and one seat was empty.

"We saved you a chair," Tom Lennox said.

"I appreciate that," Clint said, sitting and putting his money down. It appeared that most of the money already on the table had gravitated over to Lennox. "Looks like you're doing pretty well."

"Just trying to get ready for you," Lennox said. "Thought I might have to invest a bit first."

"I guess we'll see," Clint said.

"You got here just in time to deal," Lennox said, and Clint accepted the deck from the player on his right.

"Five card stud," Clint said.

***

When Amy and Nell rode into town later that afternoon, Maggie was sitting in a chair in front of her hotel. She stood up and stepped into the street. The two women reined in their horse and their buggy in front of Maggie's Hotel.

"Is he here?" Amy asked.

"He is, and I've already talked to him. He won't leave town until we meet with him."

"He knows about me?" Nell asked.

"No, so far I've only told him about Amy." Maggie looked at Amy. "Let's get her to the doctor first. His office is over here. Follow me."

Maggie walked, with Amy and Nell riding behind her. When they reached the office, Amy dismounted, and then she had Maggie helped Nell down from the buggy and took her inside.

Chapter Seven

"How is she?" Maggie asked the doctor.

Doc Evans, white-haired but not old, dried his hands with a towel and said, "She's weak. I suggest she rest here for a while, and then you take her to a hotel and get her a room. Why is she on the trail?"

"It was just something she felt had to be done," Maggie said.

"We couldn't talk her out of it, Doc," Amy said, "so we got her a buggy."

"You did the right thing, keepin' her off a horse," he said.

"She isn't bleeding, is she, Doc?" Maggie asked.

"No," he said, "but keep her off a horse. The buggy's a good idea. And make her rest in bed a few days before she starts travelin' again."

"Yessir," Amy said. "We will."

"Do you have a room?" he asked.

"I do," Maggie said, "but we'll have to get her one."

"Fine, leave her here and go do that," Evans said, "then come back and get 'er."

"We'll do that, sir," Amy said. "Thank you."

Maggie and Amy left the doctor's office and stopped just outside.

"Have you spent much time with him?" Amy asked.

Maggie hesitated, then said, "A little."

"What did you tell him?"

"Just that we had something to tell him, but I was going to wait for you to get here."

"Did you mention Nell, at all?"

"No," Maggie said, "I was saving that for us to do together."

"When?"

"Later today," Maggie said. "Let's get you and Nell registered at the hotel, first."

"How are we payin' for the hotel?" Amy asked. "You and me have no money."

"Remember," Maggie said, "Nell said she'd pay."

"I don't feel right takin' her money," Amy said.

"We're not taking it," Maggie reminded her, "she offered it."

"Yeah," Amy said, "okay."

"Come on," Maggie said, "let's put the horses and the buggy up at a livery, and then get to the hotel."

***

Once they got the horses and themselves situated, they went back to the doctor's office.

"How is she?" Maggie asked Evans.

"Asleep, but it wasn't easy. She was determined to get to her feet. I gave her something to calm her down."

"How long will she be asleep?" Amy asked.

"Probably a couple of hours. After that you can take her to the hotel."

"Thank you, Doctor," Maggie said.

"You're welcome."

They stepped outside and Maggie turned to Amy.

"Do you want to see Clint now?"

"Yes," Amy said, "we might as well let him know what's going on."

"Follow me," Maggie said, "I'm pretty sure I know where he is."

They left the doctor's office and walked a few blocks to the saloon. When they got there, Amy stopped and looked up at the sign with the establishment's name.

"'The Dead Cowboy'?" she read. "Really?"

"Why not?" Maggie said, with a shrug. "Let's go in."

"Two women with no men?" Amy asked. "Isn't that just lookin' for trouble? Remember, I worked in a saloon once."

"For a short time," Maggie reminded her. "Look, you want to talk to Clint and he's in there. When he sees us, you think he's going to let anybody bother us?"

"I hope not," Amy said. She may have worked in a saloon for a short time, but she had seen many men accost women while in a drunken stupor.

They went inside.

Both of them were dressed for travel, wearing trousers, boots and hats, but their clothing certainly didn't hide the fact that they were women. Men's eyes followed them as they walked to the bar.

"So," the bartender said, "you brought a friend, this time. You must be *lookin'* for trouble."

"Just let us have two beers," Maggie said.

The bartender shook his head. Not only did these ladies come into a saloon unaccompanied, but neither of them was even armed. He could feel the trouble brewing.

"Here ya go," he said, setting two beers down, "you better drink these and be on your way. There ain't no gentlemen in this place."

"Relax," Maggie said, "we know who we're looking for."

"Maybe you do," the bartender said, "but you don't necessarily know what you're gonna get."

Chapter Eight

Clint noticed Maggie walk in with another woman. It took a moment for him to recognize Amy Logan. They went to the bar and had a beer each. They were attracting attention, especially from four men seated at a table across the room. Clint decided to play one more hand before joining them.

***

The four men were from the nearby Templar Ranch.

"You boys see what I see?" Ted Vincent asked.

"Yeah, women," Dave Harkey answered. "So?"

"Women in a saloon, and they're not saloon girls," Vincent said. "Why do you think they're here?"

"Who cares?" Harkey answered.

"I do," Vincent said. "Come on."

The other two men, the Finch brothers, Carl and Felix, simply stood up and followed, because that's what they did. Harkey rolled his eyes and did the same.

***

As the four men approached the women, Maggie looked over at Clint. He seemed engrossed in his poker hand.

"Get ready," Maggie said.

"Don't worry," Amy said. "I've handled men like this before."

"Yes, when you were a saloon girl," Maggie said.

"I haven't forgotten how."

The four men formed a semi-circle around the women and one of them smiled.

"Ladies," he said, "welcome to Big Fork and the Dead Cowboy Saloon."

"Are you the welcoming committee?" Amy asked.

"Yeah, that's it," the man said. "We're the welcoming committee. I'm Ted, and these are my friends. We work at the Templar Ranch."

"Congratulations," Maggie said. "If you don't mind, we'd like to drink our beers in peace."

Maggie and Amy turned their backs and leaned on the bar. Vincent reached out and put his hand on Maggie's rear. Maggie turned quickly and slapped him. The saloon was noisy, so only those closest to the action heard the slap.

And Clint.

"You bitch!" Vincent snapped.

"Keep your hands to yourself!" she snapped at him.

Vincent started to reach for her throat but heard a voice that stopped him.

"You heard the lady," Clint said. "Hands off."

Vincent stopped with his hands inches from Maggie's throat and turned his head. He saw Clint standing there, recognized him as one of the poker players, but didn't know his name.

"Mister," Dave Harkey said, "you should mind your own business."

Clint looked at the four men. Two of them were tall, skinny and young, looked like brothers. The one who had just spoken to him was a very large man in his thirties. And the one who had put his hand on Maggie's ass was in his thirties, stood about six feet but looked a bit undernourished.

Clint spoke to the big man.

"You should teach your friend some manners," he said. "That's no way to act around a lady."

"You think these two are ladies?" Ted Vincent asked. "They're in a saloon without any men escorting them. Whataya think they're lookin' for?"

"I happen to know what they're looking for," Clint said.

"Oh yeah?" Vincent asked. "What's that?"

"Me."

"So they're your women?" Vincent asked.

"They're my friends," Clint said. "You're interrupting their drinking, and my poker game. Now you and your friends run along."

"Run along?" Harkey asked. He didn't agree with Vincent's idea to approach these women, but he didn't like being spoken to that way. "Who the hell do you think you are?"

"I just told you," Clint said. "I'm they're friend, and the man whose poker game you just interrupted."

"Well," Dave Harkey said, turning to face Clint head on, "why don't you go back to your game and leave us to entertain these . . . ladies?"

Clint saw that all four men were wearing sidearms, but they were wearing them the same way they wore hats and boots. None of the four had any idea how to properly use the guns. They were, after all, cowpokes.

But Harkey was a big, powerfully built man, and he was the one Clint decided he needed to be wary of.

"You seem to be the one with some sense," Clint said to him. "Why not take your friends outside so they can live to be foolish another day."

"You threatenin' our lives?" Harkey demanded. "Is that what you're doin', friend?"

"You men should leave," Amy said. "You don't want to do this."

"You shut up!" Vincent shouted. "My friend's gonna give your friend some advice, the hard way."

Dave Harkey rubbed his hands together, then cracked his knuckles.

"You think I'm going to fight you?" Clint asked.

"Whatsamatta?" Harkey asked. "You chicken?"

"No," Clint said, "I'm smart, unlike the four of you. I'll put a bullet between your eyes before I let you lay your paws on me."

"Paws?"

"Yeah," Clint said, "paws, like a damn, dirty ape."

Harkey flexed his fingers.

"You know," Clint said, "you really shouldn't wear a gun when all you know how to do is punch cows."

Vincent and the Finch brothers all turned to face Clint, with Harkey.

"You do know there's four of us, right?" Vincent asked.

"That's okay," Clint said, "I've got six bullets."

The four men exchanged puzzled glances.

"This man's crazy," Harkey said.

"He's not crazy," Amy said.

"He's the Gunsmith," Maggie said.

Now all four men looked at Clint, again.

"That's a lie," Harkey said.

"No, it ain't," the bartender said. "He's Clint Adams, and he's been playin' poker in here for days. You fellas better move along. I don't want your blood all over my saloon."

"Ted," one of the Finch brothers started.

"Dave," Vincent said, putting his hand on Harkey's arm. "Let's go. These two bitches ain't worth it."

"Yeah, we'll go," Harkey said, then looked at Clint and added, "but I'll find you when you ain't wearin' that gun, Mister."

"That's not likely, friend," Clint said.

Vincent closed his hand on Harkey's arm and pulled.

"Hang on," Clint said, as the men started to leave.

"What" Vincent asked.

"You apologize to the lady for disrespecting her," Clint said to him.

Vincent stared at Clint a few moments, then turned to Maggie and said, "Sorry, Ma'am, for disrepectin' you."

"Yeah, it's fine," Maggie said. "Just go while you still can."

As Vincent turned to follow the Finch boys out of the saloon. Harkey looked at Clint again.

"Remember what I said."

"Come *on*, Dave!" Vincent said, and yanked on his friend's arm until they were out the batwing doors.

Clint looked at Maggie and Amy and said, "Hello, ladies." Then he said to the bartender, "Three more beers."

Chapter Nine

"Hello, Amy," Clint said.

"Hello, Clint," she said. "It's good to see you."

"Maggie tells me you two have been looking for me," he said. "Now that we're all together, maybe you can tell me why?"

"Can we go someplace more quiet?" Maggie asked.

"The café across the street?" he asked.

"Sounds good," Maggie said.

"Then let's go."

He paid for the fresh beers, and then they left them on the bar and took their leave . . .

***

In the café they ordered coffee and pie and sat virtually alone in the empty place.

"Well, ladies," Clint said, "here we are."

"We're here with someone else," Amy said.

"And who's that?" Clint asked.

"Nell Livingston," Maggie said.

"Who?"

"You don't remember Nell?" Amy asked.

"Nell," Clint said, thinking.

"I know you've met a lot of women over the years, Clint," Maggie said. "But you seem to have an amazing memory."

"Well, maybe it's just the name I don't remember," Clint suggested.

"Right," Amy said, "maybe you'll know her when you see her."

"And when will she be getting to town?" Clint asked.

"She's here," Amy said, "but right now she's over at the doctor's office."

"Was she injured?"

"Sick is more like it," Maggie said. "She really shouldn't have traveled, but she insisted on it. But the doctor treated her, and he says she'll be fine after she gets some rest."

"We're supposed to go over there and bring her to the hotel," Amy said.

"I can help with that," Clint said.

"No," Maggie said, "I think we should let her rest, maybe all night, before she sits down with you. It'll do her some good."

"All right," he said. "I'll see Nell tomorrow, then. Meanwhile, you two can tell me why you've been looking for me."

"Well," Amy said, "that really has to do with Nell, so we should let her tell you."

"Then what will you do with the rest of today?" he asked.

"To tell you the truth," Amy said, "we could use some rest, too. At least, I could."

"I could, too," Maggie said, giving Clint a warning look. Obviously, she didn't want Amy to know they had been together the night before.

"Then you ladies get your rest," he said, "and we'll have breakfast together tomorrow morning in your hotel."

They all agreed.

Chapter Ten

Three years earlier . . .

The Logan ranch was situated several miles outside of Tannerville, Wyoming.

Clint rode in, looking for water for both himself and his Darley Arabian, Eclipse. There was a well on the property, but he didn't approach it. He didn't want to assume anything and maybe have somebody come out of the house with a rifle to run him off. His intention was to ask if he could water his horse.

So he rode toward the well but stopped and kept his eye on the house. He thought he saw the curtain in the window move, and assumed he was being watched.

"Hello, the house!" he called out.

There was no answer. He took off his hat and wiped the sweat off his forehead with his shirt sleeve before replacing it.

"My horse and I could sure use some water!" he called.

Again, no answer. But then the door opened a crack—just wide enough for someone to push a rifle barrel through, if they wanted to.

"You can go ahead and use the well," a woman's voice said.

"Thank you, Ma'am."

"But then you've got to be on your way."

"No problem," he said, then repeated, "Thank you."

He rode Eclipse up to the well and dismounted. He sent the wooden bucket down, wound it back up and used the metal cup that was hanging on a nail to scoop some out and drank. Then he held the bucket out for Eclipse to drink his fill.

Amy later told him that she had watched him and the Darley Arabian together and was impressed. That was why she decided to come out of the house.

"Is he hungry?" she asked.

Clint turned, saw a tall, slender, pretty woman standing just in front of the door.

"I'm sure he is," Clint said.

"And you?"

"Definitely."

"Why don't you take him to the barn and feed him," she said, "then come into the house and I'll feed you."

"That's very generous."

She went back inside.

Clint took Eclipse to the barn, unsaddled him, rubbed him down, and then fed him.

"There you go, big boy," he said, "enjoy."

He left the barn and walked to the house. When he entered, she was at the stove, and turned to face him.

"Please, sit at the table," she said. "Coffee, or something stronger?"

"Coffee's fine." He sat.

She set a tarnished cup in front of him and then went back to the stove. Next time she came to the table she brought a bowl of stew and a basket of bread.

"Thank you," he said.

She sat across from him.

"Aren't you going to eat?" he asked.

"Not yet," she said. "I used to enjoy watching my husband eat."

"Where is he?"

"He died several years ago," she said. "I've been trying to keep the ranch going on my own since then."

"It must be very hard."

"It is. Do you mind if I watch you eat?"

"Not at all," he said, breaking off a hunk of bread and dipping it into the stew.

They talked while he ate, and later that night they ended up in her bed together. She was a slightly built woman, with small breasts but large nipples. Her skin was remarkably smooth. He loved running his fingertips over it, and then his lips and tongue.

He stayed with her at the ranch for three days, doing some repairs, letting Eclipse rest, letting her watch him eat, and sharing her bed. When he finally left, she thanked him and watched him ride off until he was out of sight . . .

***

The present . . .

"What are you doing?" Maggie asked Amy, the next morning.

They were in the hotel dining room with Clint, having breakfast.

"Oh," Amy said, "sorry, I was just watching him eat."

She picked up her fork and started eating her own breakfast.

Clint had spent the night trying to remember a woman named Nell Livingston. No matter how hard he tried, he couldn't bring her to mind. He hoped when he saw her it would all come back to him. Usually, he didn't have trouble remembering people.

"Is Nell coming down for breakfast?" Clint asked.

"We told her we'd bring something up to her," Maggie said.

"What are we bringing her?" he asked.

"Breakfast," Amy said, "and you."

Chapter Eleven

After breakfast they ordered a plate for Nell and carried it up to the room. Maggie used the key to unlock the door.

"Nell," she said, as they entered, "we brought you breakfast, and a visitor."

The girl on the bed had been lying with her back to the door. Now she rolled over and looked at them.

"Nell," Amy said, "we brought Clint to see you."

She stared at Clint, and he stared back.

"That's not Clint," Nell said.

"I don't know this woman," Clint said. "Never saw her before."

"Wait a minute," Maggie said, looking at Nell. "You said you slept with Clint Adams, and he was the father of your baby."

"What?"

"That's right," Nell said, "but this isn't the man I slept with."

Maggie and Amy looked at each other, helplessly.

"Give the girl her breakfast," Clint suggested, "and then let's see if we can get to the bottom of this."

***

It became fairly obvious that a man had come to Nell Livingston's town, claiming to be Clint Adams, the Gunsmith. He took her to bed, left town and got her pregnant. After the birth of the child, Maggie and Amy came to town, met her after exchanging stories, decided to try and help her.

"We wanted to find you," Maggie said, "and determine if you actually were her baby's father."

"We even named ourselves," Amy said, looking chagrined. "We called ourselves 'The Gunsmith Women's Club.'"

Clint looked at Nell, who was avidly eating the breakfast they had brought her.

"I'm sorry this happened to you," he said. "And I'm sorry you're ill."

"She just decided to travel too soon after the baby's birth," Maggie said. "She's too weak."

"And now I'll have to go home and tell my parents how stupid I was to be fooled by a man who lied to me," she said.

"Nell, how old are you?" Clint asked.

"Nineteen."

"So you were eighteen when you met this man," Clint said. "And how old was he?"

"I don't know," she said. "He was older than me, but not as old as you." She looked embarrassed. "I guess that should've been my first clue that he was lying. He wasn't old enough to be the Gunsmith."

Clint looked at Maggie and Amy.

"What do you ladies intend to do now?"

"We'll have to take her back home," Maggie said. "We can't just leave her alone."

"I'll tell you what I'd like to do," Amy said. "I'd like to find the man who lied to her, make him apologize to her . . ."

"And be a father to her baby," Maggie added.

"I think I've had enough of playing poker here," Clint said. "Do you mind if I ride back with you?"

"Why would you do that?" Nell asked. "You don't owe me anythin'."

"I'm not very happy that a man did this to you, using my name," Clint explained. "Maybe I can find him."

"That would be wonderful!" Nell gushed.

Clint looked at Maggie and Amy.

"Let me know when you want to start out," he said.

"We should give her another day to rest," Maggie said. "How about tomorrow morning?"

"That'll be fine," Clint said. "I'll be ready."

He started for the door.

"I'll walk you down," Maggie said.

When they got to the lobby, she put her hand on his arm to stop him.

"I don't think you should come to my room tonight," she said. "Not with Amy down the hall."

"All right."

"And . . . I suppose you could go to Amy's room, if you wanted," she said. "It would only be fair."

"I think I'll just stay in my room at the boarding house, until morning," he said. "That might be safer."

"I told you," she said, "I'm not the jealous type."

"Still," he said, "just to be on the safe side."

"Whatever you say."

"By the way," he said, "where does Nell live?"

"A town in southern Wyoming called Collinsville." Maggie had lived in northern Wyoming.

"I've never been there," he said.

"It's small," she said. "In fact, Nell lives with her parents outside of town."

"And where's the baby?"

"She left it with her mother," Maggie said. "It's a little boy."

"Well," Clint said, "let's see what we can do about getting this little boy a father."

She kissed his cheek, said, "You're a good man," and went back upstairs.

Chapter Twelve

Clint went to the Dead Cowboy Saloon that night to play a few hands and let the players know he'd be leaving town the next morning.

"Guess that means I better win as much of your money as I can tonight," Lennox said.

"Good luck," Clint said.

"Speaking of luck," Lennox said, "isn't that the fella who had this chair before me by the bar? He keeps starin' over here."

"He don't have the money to buy back in," one of the other players said. "He's still not happy about Mr. Adams, here, cleanin' him out."

"You shouldn't play poker if you can't take gettin' cleaned out every once in a while," Lennox said.

"He don't get that," the other man said.

"And he's wearin' a gun," Lennox said. "I didn't see him wearin' one yesterday."

"I noticed that, too," Clint said. "I might be leaving town just in time, before he gets the nerve to try and use that gun."

"You can't be afraid of a kid with a gun," Lennox said.

"I'm just afraid I may have to kill him," Clint clari-
fied.

"Oh, now that I can see."

"In fact," Clint said, "if I was in my room instead of
here, I wouldn't have to give him a thought."

"Don't let some sore loser kid keep me from takin'
your money, Adams," Lennox said, smiling.

"I guess I'll stay around just to give you some les-
sons," Clint said.

"There you go," Lennox said. "Jacks or better."

***

Clint learned a lot about playing poker from some
expert players. Bat Masterson taught him not to play
every hand. Doc Holliday once told him all you had to do
to be successful was win every other hand. Brady
Hawkes once told him not to change his style of play
according to the stakes. High or low stakes, play your
game. But the two brothers, Bret and Bart, had given him
the same piece of advice at different times. You want to
beat the other player, but there's no point in humiliating
him at the same time.

Tom Lennox had one thing going for him. Win or
lose, he seemed to have the same temperament. It was as
if he was just happy to be playing.

After a couple of hours Clint and Lennox had most of the money on the table in front of them. The other players dropped out one-by-one, and now there was only one more.

"Well," he said, "I guess I might as well bet the rest of what I've got. This is my first decent hand in an hour." He pushed the remainder of his money into the pot. "I raise forty dollars."

"Well," Lennox said, "since that's all you've got left, I'll just call ya."

"Same here," Clint said, shoving forty into the pot.

"Straight to the Ace," the man said, laying his cards down.

"Flush," Lennox said, "All hearts."

"Full house," Clint said, "Eights over threes."

"That's it for me, gents," the third player said. "Mr. Adams. I can't say I'm sorry that you're leavin' in the mornin'. No offense."

"None taken," Clint assured him.

The man grabbed his coat and hat and took his leave.

"And then there were two," Lennox said. "Should we even bother head-to-head? We could be at it all night."

The stakes of the game were not huge. Walking out of the Dead Cowboy Saloon without any of the money would not break either man.

"How about one hand," Clint suggested. "Winner takes all?"

"Sure," Lennox said, "but let's make it seven card stud."

"Why not?" Clint asked, handing him the deck. "It's your deal."

"All seven cards face up?" Lennox asked. "After all, no betting, no strategy, right? Just luck."

"Right," Clint said, "just luck."

Lennox started to deal, and after they each had six cards on the table, neither of them had a pair.

"I have King high," Lennox said, "and you have Queen high. If one of us doesn't pair up on the seventh card, I win."

"I guess we'll see, won't we?" Clint asked.

"I guess we will."

Lennox dealt Clint his seventh card and paired deuces.

"Well, well," Lennox said. "Any pair I get will beat that."

"If you get a pair."

Lennox stared across the table at Clint, put the deck down.

"Odds are I'll get a pair," he said.

"There's only one way we're going to find out," Clint told him.

"Right," Lennox said. He picked up the deck and dealt himself a seventh card.

"Shit," he said.

Chapter Thirteen

"You took my seat."

Lennox looked up from his mismatched seven cards while Clint raked in the pot. Uriah Happ had walked over from the bar and was glaring at him.

"What?"

"You took my seat," Happ said.

"No, he didn't," Clint said. "You lost and had to leave the table."

"I ain't talkin' to you," Happ said, "I'm talkin' to him." He pointed at Lennox. "I'm gonna wait for you outside."

"What?" Lennox asked.

"You heard me," Happ said. "When you come out, you better be wearin' a gun."

"I—I don't wear a gun," Lennox said. "I'm a gambler, not a gunman."

"You better get a gun from somewhere, then," Happ said, "because I'll be waitin' on the street."

He turned and walked out of the saloon.

"What the hell—" Lennox said. "First, I lose all my money to you, and now he wants to kill me? I'm not havin' a good day."

"Go out the back door," Clint said. "Avoid him."

"Will I be able to avoid him forever?" Lennox asked.

"Go out the back and leave town," Clint said. "You have no reason to go out and meet him."

"Is that what you'd do?"

"No," Clint said, "I'd have no choice but to go out the front. But that's because of who I am. You don't have that problem."

"I don't know, Mr. Adams," Lennox said. "I don't like the idea of runnin'. Maybe I can talk to him, make him see how foolish he's bein'. Make him see he's wrong. I didn't take his seat, like you said."

"I wouldn't go out those doors without a gun if I was you, Mr. Lennox."

"It wouldn't do any good for me to have a gun," Lennox said. "I can't shoot worth a tinker's damn."

"Well," Clint said, putting his money away, "maybe he's not serious."

"He's serious."

They both turned and looked at the bartender. The saloon was mostly empty, so the man had been able to hear everything that had occurred.

"What's that?" Clint asked.

"Happ fancies himself a fast gun," the bartender said. "He's always challenging men to meet him in the street."

"And?" Clint asked.

The bartender shrugged.

"He kills most of them."

"Why challenge Mr. Lennox, here, and not me?" Clint asked.

"He may not think he's ready for you," the bartender said. "Or maybe you're just next."

"After me," Lennox added.

"Well, then," Clint said, "I'll just go out the door before you, and we'll see what happens."

"And what do I do?" Lennox asked.

Clint stood up.

"Just wait."

Clint walked to the batwing doors, watched by the few men who were drinking this early. As he went through the doors, they all hurried to the windows.

***

When Happ saw Clint come out of the saloon, he wasn't happy.

"Where is he?" he demanded. "Where's the sonofabitch who stole my chair?"

"Nobody stole your chair, Happ," Clint said. "And even if he did, a chair is nothing to die over."

"I don't plan to die."

"Okay," Clint said, "then a chair is nothing to kill over, either."

"I can't let somebody get away with that," Happ said. "People will think they can take what's mine any time they want."

"Don't be an ass, kid," Clint said.

"What?"

"You heard me. Lennox isn't coming out, and you're going to turn and walk away."

"Are you threatening me, Adams?"

"I suppose I am," Clint said. "Lennox is a good poker player, and you're a bad one. You should never sit down at a poker table."

Happ firmed his jaw.

"I ain't walkin' away," he said. "If Lennox ain't comin' out, you better be ready to use that gun. And since he ain't got a gun, he might as well take yours from your dead body when he comes out."

"Now you're just being stupid," Clint said. The street had emptied out, but people were standing at their doors and windows, watching the action, waiting for someone to die.

"These people want blood, kid," Clint said, "and you're giving them what they want."

Chapter Fourteen

"There's nobody on the street," Happ said.

"Oh, don't worry," Clint said. "They're watching. Just take a look."

Happ didn't bother.

"They're always watchin' when I'm out here," he said. "Only this time they're gonna see me really add to my reputation. See, I knew you wouldn't let that gambler come out and face me."

Clint studied Happ for a moment, then said, "That's pretty good. I hate being that predictable, but it was pretty good. You're right, I wouldn't just let you kill Lennox."

"So here we are," Happ said. "You took my money, so I'm going to take your life."

"Happ," Clint said, "you're making a big mistake."

"If I am," Happ said, "I guess it'll be my last."

Clint decided to get it over with. Instead of waiting for Happ to move first, he drew and fired. He sent one bullet into the young man's chest, knocking him onto his back. He was dead before he hit the ground.

Lennox shouted through the batwing doors.

"Can I come out now?" he asked. "Is it safe?"

Clint walked to Happ, checked the body to be sure he was dead, then said to Lennox, "It's safe."

He ejected the spent shell, replaced it and holstered the gun.

"Uh-oh," Lennox said, coming up alongside him. "Here comes the law. Do you know him?"

"I met him when I came to town," Clint said, "haven't talked to him since."

People started coming out onto the street, talking and pointing.

"Well, look at you," the sheriff said. "If you had to kill one person while you were in here, this was the right one."

"You mean you're not going to kick me out of town?" Clint asked.

"Not for killin' Uriah Happ," the sheriff said. "The Mayor will probably want to give you a medal."

"Was he that much trouble?"

"A royal pain," the sheriff said. "Must've killed at least six men."

"Why didn't you lock him up after the first?" Clint asked.

"He's got family," the lawman said, "and if anyone from town killed him, they would've burned it to the ground."

"And now?"

"Well," the lawman said, "now you killed him, not the town. So they'll be comin' after you."

"When?"

"Pretty soon."

"I'm leaving tomorrow," Clint said.

"Well," the sheriff said, "they'll come after you."

"It's like that?"

The sheriff nodded.

"It's like that."

"How many?"

"Father, brothers, uncles, cousins . . . there are quite a few Happs."

"That would've been nice to know before I killed him," Clint said.

"Why?"

"I would've figured some other way to take care of him," Clint said.

The sheriff looked down at the dead man.

"Naw, this one worked just fine."

"Why do I feel like I've been suckered?"

The sheriff laughed and walked off, shaking his head.

Was this the plan all along? To get the Gunsmith to do their dirty work for them? Clint remembered when Happ walked into the saloon, approached the table and put his money down on it. It was like he knew he was expected.

"So what now?" Lennox asked,

"Now I leave town tomorrow, like I said."

"And if his relatives come after you?"

"I'll deal with that when the time comes," he told Lennox. "What about you?"

They got off the street to talk in front of the saloon.

"If the Happs show up tomorrow, it'll be a big day for this town. Maybe I'll just watch."

"You'll want to watch from cover," Clint said.

"You sayin' there's definitely gonna be trouble?"

"I can almost guarantee it," Clint said. "Especially if anyone tries to keep me from leaving."

"Yeah, well," Lennox said, "like I figured, it might be worth getting up early to watch."

"We'll see," Clint said. "Going back inside?"

"Why not?" Lennox said. "I'm sure there's still some beer left, and a few new card players might come in."

"I thought I won all your money?" Clint said, with a grin.

"Just the money I had on the table," Lennox said. He tossed Clint a salute and went back into the saloon.

Clint turned, saw the sheriff ushering people away from the body so a few men could pick it up and take it to the undertaker. He turned and walked the other way.

Chapter Fifteen

The next morning, he met the three women in the lobby, after saying goodbye to his landlady.

"I thought you'd be staying longer," she complained. "I thought we had . . . time."

He touched her face and said, "I wouldn't want to be the reason you leave the Church, Kate."

"I wouldn't leave my church for you, you fool," she said. "Just maybe bend a commandment or two." She smiled.

"I'm sorry," he said. "I just couldn't wait that long."

As he walked away, disappointment etched onto her lovely face.

Maggie and Amy stood with Nell between them. It almost looked as if they were holding her up.

"Breakfast?" Clint asked.

"Why not?" Maggie asked.

They went into the dining room and all ordered ham-and-eggs and coffee.

"How are you feeling?" Clint asked Nell.

"Still foolish," she said.

"Well, we're going to fix that," he said.

"Why?"

"Excuse me?"

"Why are you gonna help me?" she asked. "You don't owe me nothin'."

"But the man who got you pregnant in my name, he owes us both," Clint said. "After this we'll go to the livery, saddle up, hitch up the buggy and get going."

"Your mother will be happy to see you," Maggie said to Nell.

"And I'll be happy to see little Clint."

"Little Clint?" Clint repeated.

"Well . . . when I thought his father was Clint Adams, I named him . . . I can change it."

"There's no reason to change the little tyke's name," Clint said. "It's always served me well."

They all started to eat their breakfast.

***

They traveled slowly, keeping to Nell's pace. Maggie and Amy took turns cooking each night they camped.

Because the sheriff had warned him about the Happ family, Clint decided to stay on watch each night. He allowed the ladies to sleep, took some cat naps himself, depending on Eclipse to let him know if anyone was coming close to camp.

On the last night, Maggie sat up a while with Clint.

"We should make Collinsville by noon tomorrow," Clint said.

"I think Nell would rather go right to her parent's house," Maggie said. "That should add about another hour to the ride."

"No problem," Clint said. "If that's where her baby is, that's where she should be."

"You know," she said, "you've taken this all very well. I mean, a man impersonating you gets a girl pregnant, she names her baby after you . . . most men would have reacted very differently."

"It's not her fault," he said, "and it sure as hell isn't the child's fault. And why shouldn't he be named Clint? It's a good name."

"Did you go to Amy's room the last night in town?" she asked, suddenly changing the subject.

"What?"

"I'm just—"

"—jealous?"

"No," she said, "I told you I'm not the jealous type. I'm . . . curious."

"Did you ask her?"

"No!" Maggie said. "I wouldn't do that."

"Why not?"

"We're friends, now," she said. "I wouldn't want her to think I was accusing her of anything."

"You know," Clint said, "since you two are friends, I should probably stay away from both of you."

"Well," Maggie said, "I don't think either one of us wants to go that far. Maybe we could just . . . share you."

"Let's see what happens," Clint suggested. "I may be out chasing down this phony Clint Adams. Why don't you get some sleep? We'll leave early tomorrow morning."

"Whatever you say."

She stood up and walked to her bedroll.

There hadn't been any sign of anyone following them during the day or approaching their camp at night, but he decided to go ahead and stand watch, anyway.

***

The next morning Clint decided they should only have coffee and then move on. None of the women argued, and Nell seemed very anxious to get moving.

Eventually, they stopped that afternoon in front of a small house that was in need of some repair. The fence, aside from falling down, needed a coat of paint, as did the entire house. And Clint could see some places in the roof that desperately needed patching.

"This is it?" Clint asked.

"It used to look nice," Nell said. "Then my father got too old to keep it up."

"And your mother?"

"She's a little younger than Pa, but she don't do this kinda work," Nell explained. "She's real good with little Clint, though."

"That's good," Amy said.

"Yeah," Nell said, "yeah, it is."

Clint helped her down from the buggy.

"Do you want us to come in with you?" he asked.

"No, I better go in alone," Nell said. "I have some explainin' to do." She looked at the three of them. "But if you could come back tonight for supper?"

"Sure," Clint said. "We can do that. We'll get situated in a hotel in town and see you later."

Nell hugged both Maggie and Amy tightly, stared at Clint awkwardly, then turned and walked to the front of the house. They waited until she got inside before mounting up and riding to town.

Chapter Sixteen

In Collinsville, a small town, they stopped in front of the Brass Cartridge Hotel.

"We stayed here last time we were here," Maggie said. "It's clean."

"Fine by me," Clint said.

They went inside and got two rooms, one for the two women, one for Clint.

"I'll take the horses to the stable," Clint said. "You ladies get some rest."

"But we'll need the horses to go back to the house," Amy said.

"They need some rest, too," Clint said, "but they'll be ready."

He left them in their room and took the horses to what he thought was the closest livery stable. It turned out it was the only stable in town.

He carried his rifle and saddlebags back to the hotel and set them on the bed. As he did, one opened and the book he was currently reading slid out. *The Merry Adventures of Robin Hood,* an 1883 novel by a man named Howard Pyle. Actually, he'd been meaning to start it for some time but had been carrying it around for weeks now. He decided to read a few pages while waiting til it was time to go to supper.

***

A hundred pages later, he looked at the time and was surprised to see how much had gone by. He put the book down, washed up, put on a clean shirt and walked down the hall to Maggie and Amy's room.

Maggie answered his knock on their door.

"Ready?" he asked.

"The horses?"

"We can pick them up at the livery."

"Then let's go," Amy said from inside the room. "I'm hungry."

***

When they got to the house, they dismounted and stood out front.

"Should we knock on the door?" Amy asked.

"I suppose—" Maggie started, but at that moment the door opened, and Nell stepped out.

"I've been waitin' for you," she said. "Come on in."

The three of them walked to the door and followed Nell inside, single file, with Clint last.

"Is this him?" a man demanded. He was tall, elderly, with white hair and a wrinkled face. "Is this the bastard?"

"No, Pa," Nell said. "This ain't him. This is the real Clint Adams."

"Real one, huh?" Nell's father gave Clint a curious look.

"Where's the baby?" Maggie asked.

"Yeah," Amy said, "we wanna see him."

"This way," Nell said. "My Ma's got him."

As Maggie and Amy followed Nell, her father said to Clint, "Not you. We got some talkin' to do."

"Go ahead," Clint told the women.

"You may not be the bastard that got my daughter in family way," the man said, "but he used your name. What do you intend to do about that? A man needs to defend his honor—his good name."

"Well, Mr. Livingston," Clint said. "I intend to find him and bring him back here."

"Good," the man said, "then he can pay what he owes me."

"I'm going to make sure he pays Nell what he owes her," Clint said, "not you."

"Same difference."

"I think you'll end up seeing that it's not," Clint told him. "Now if you'll excuse me, I'd like to see my little namesake."

Chapter Seventeen

Maggie and Amy fussed over the baby while Nell and her mother got supper on the table. Then, as they ate, Nell remained in the bedroom with the child. Her mother brought a plate in to her.

Her father's name was Noble Livingston, and her mother was Mildred. Clint found it odd that the couple had such opposite sounding names, one simple, and one grand.

As it turned out, her mother was a terrible cook, but they all ate without making any negative comments. Clint was also surprised that, during the meal, her mother did all the talking while her father remained silent. She asked Maggie, Amy and Clint all the same questions, such as where they were from, what they were doing, what they wanted from life.

"Right now, Mrs. Livingston—" Clint started.

"Oh, honey, just call me Mildred, everybody does."

"Mildred," Clint went on, "what I want to do now is find the man who lied to your daughter and told her he was me."

"And you want to do this for your benefit, or hers?" Mildred asked.

"To me, it's all the same," Clint answered.

"I see." She took her napkin from her lap, set in on the table and stood. "I'm gonna check on Nell."

As she left the room, the table fell silent. Noble did not seem to be in the mood for any conversation. When Mildred returned, she had Nell's plate, only half empty, with her, and began to clear the table.

"Let us help," Maggie said. She And Amy stood and began to clean.

"Mr. Adams," Noble said, "join me outside for a cigar?"

"Thank you, I will," Clint said.

He didn't usually smoke, but when someone offered him a cigar, it was usually some sort of gesture, so he often accepted.

Outside on the dilapidated porch, they lit their cigar and smoked standing up.

"This used to be a nice place," Noble said. "Before I got old and useless, I'd keep it up. Now it's just fallin' to shit."

"I might be able to do some work for you while I'm here," Clint offered.

"The work you're gonna do is to catch that bastard who abused my daughter," Noble said. "And I'd like you to either kill 'im, or bring him here so I can do it."

"Mr. Livingston," Clint said, "I'm going to make sure he knows I don't take kindly to people using my name, and I'll bring him here so Nell can have her say. Beyond that, I'm afraid I won't be able to help you."

"Don't you kill people?" Noble asked. "Ain't that what you do?"

"When they don't leave me a choice, yes," Clint admitted.

"Well, hopefully he won't give you a choice," Noble said.

Maggie and Amy came out of the house.

"I think we should go," Maggie said.

"I need to talk to Nell about the phony me," Clint said.

"We can do that tomorrow, can't we?" Amy asked.

"Sure," Clint said, "why not? Good night, Mr. Livingston. Please thank your wife for the supper."

Noble grumbled something. Clint, Maggie and Amy mounted their horses and headed back to town. There wasn't much conversation forthcoming from the two ladies, so Clint decided to leave it until they reached their destination.

***

As they dismounted and handed their mounts to the hostler at the livery, Maggie asked, "What did you and Nell's father talk about?"

"He wants me to kill the man when I find him," Clint said. "Or else, bring him back so he can do it."

"What did you tell him?" Amy asked.

"That's not what I do," Clint answered.

"What *are* you going to do?" Maggie asked. "I mean, when you find him?"

"Just what I told Nell's father," Clint said. "I'll let him know I'm not happy with him, make sure he never impersonates me again, and then bring him to Nell so she can say what she wants to say."

"I don't know that she'll say anything," Maggie said, as they started walking to the hotel. "She feels pretty foolish about the whole thing."

"Well," Clint said, "maybe by the time I find the man and bring him back, she'll muster some anger."

"I hope so," Amy said. "I want her to stand up for herself."

"I guess we'll have to wait and see," Maggie said.

When they reached the hotel, Clint walked with Maggie and Amy to their door.

"We're going to turn in early," Maggie said. "How about you? Going to the saloon?"

"I don't think so," Clint said. "I'd like to get some rest, too. Tomorrow I'm going to have to start looking for this man."

"We'll say good night, then," Maggie said. She and Amy went into the room, and Clint walked to his.

Chapter Eighteen

Clint was reading *Robin Hood* when the knock came at his door. It wasn't a timid knock, which led him to believe it was a man, not a woman. But in either case he would have done the same thing, take his gun to the door with him and stand to one side.

"Who is it?"

"Mr. Adams?" a man said. "I'm Sheriff Brett. I'd like to talk to you."

Clint cracked the door, looked out and saw the man with the badge. Then he opened the door wider to take a better look. Sheriff Brett was middle-aged, about five nine with a flabby middle and a pale complexion.

"Mr. Adams?"

"That's right."

Brett looked down at the gun in Clint's hand.

"You mind if I come in?"

"Sure, why not?" Clint said, backing away.

"Thank you." Brett entered, and took off his hat. The first thing Clint noticed was the man's big ears.

Instead of walking back to the bed and holstering his gun, Clint tucked it into his belt.

"What can I do for you, Sheriff?"

"I heard you were in town," he said, "and I heard some talk, so I wanted to check it out."

"What kind of talk?"

"Well," Brett said, "folks are sayin' you're here to kill somebody."

"Is that what they're saying?"

"Is it true?"

"No."

"But weren't you out at the Livingston place?"

"I was," Clint said. "So?"

"So Noble Livingston's been talkin' for weeks how some man took advantage of his daughter, and he wanted to see him dead. I guess folks thought you were here because he hired you."

"Then folks haven't been listening," Clint said. "Nell and her family thought I was the one who had taken advantage of her, until we all found out that somebody was impersonating me."

"Impersonatin' you?" Brett asked.

"You never heard about that?"

"Not a word."

"Then I suppose when he was here, he wasn't impersonating me all over town, but just with Nell Livingston."

"If there was a man in town sayin' he was you, I woulda talked to him, just like I'm talkin' to you. In fact, how do I know you're really Clint Adams?"

"Well," Clint said, "I'm a little tired tonight, but if you want me to shoot somebody for you tomorrow, just to prove myself—"

"That's all right," Sheriff Brett said, putting his hand up, "that won't be necessary. Thank you for takin' the time to talk to me."

"I'm not here looking for trouble, Sheriff," Clint said. "But I am here looking for the man who was claiming to be me."

"Well," Sheriff Brett said, "I can't say I blame ya for that. Good night to you, sir." He put his hat back on and left the room.

Clint walked to the bed, slid his gun back into the holster hanging there. This was a small town, so word was going to get out fast that he was there, and why. If the impersonator was within earshot, he might clear out. Even without the talk, once he'd registered at the hotel, word had probably gotten out.

He got himself situated on the bed again, with his back against the bedpost, and went back to *Robin Hood* and his merry men.

***

When Sheriff Brett entered his office, the man sitting at his desk asked, "Did you talk to him?"

"Yeah, I did," Brett said. "Now get the hell out of my chair."

The younger man stood up, and Brett sat heavily, with a sigh.

"What did he say?"

"He said he's gonna find the man who impersonated him and make him pay."

"Shit!"

"I told you no good would come from callin' yourself Clint Adams, didn't I?" Brett asked. "I warned you."

"Yeah, yeah," the younger man said, "my big brother is always tellin' me what I should and shouldn't do."

"That's right," Sheriff Brett said, "and now I'm tellin' you to get outta town."

"Look," Simon Brett said, "when I came here, you said I could stay with you."

"That was before you met Nell Livingston and told her you were Clint Adams, although I don't know why in hell she'd believe you. You're obviously not old enough."

"I was older than her," Simon said. "That was all she knew."

"Simon—"

"I don't get it," Simon said, cutting him off. "Why didn't you just kill Adams when you had the chance."

"I can't just kill a man," Sheriff Dan Brett said. "I'm the sheriff."

"Exactly," Simon said. "You're the law in this town and everybody would believe you didn't have a choice. He's the goddamn Gunsmith."

"I didn't have the chance, Simon," the sheriff said, quickly.

"As soon as he opened the door—"

"He was holdin' his gun," the lawman said. "He woulda killed me."

"So your only advice is for me to leave town?"

"Yes," the sheriff said. "Let me know where you end up, and I'll send for you once I figure out what to do."

"Dan . . . we just found each other as brothers," Simon pointed out.

"And you messed it up for a poke," the sheriff reminded him.

"Hey, you've seen her," Simon argued. "She's really pretty."

"Well then," Sheriff Brett said, "I guess the only thing you have to decide is whether or not she was pretty enough to die for."

Chapter Nineteen

Clint was asleep the next time there was a knock at the door. This time it was definitely a timid knock. He grabbed his gun and padded barefoot to the door.

"Yeah, who is it?"

"Clint, quick," Amy hissed, "let me in."

"Amy?"

He opened the door and she rushed past him.

"Quick, close it!"

He closed the door, turned to look at her. She was wearing a robe over a nightgown, which was probably why she didn't want to be seen in the hall.

"What's going on?" he asked. "Where's Maggie?"

"She's asleep," Amy said. "She sleeps real soundly, so I snuck out."

"Why?" he asked.

"Why do you think?" she asked. She shrugged off her robe, which fell to the floor, and then sent the nightgown after it. She stood there naked, letting Clint take in her long, sleek nudity.

"What about Maggie?" he asked.

"Oh, she won't wake up," Amy said. "Don't worry." She walked up to him, put her hands on his chest. "It's been a long time."

"Yes, it has." He put his left hand on her smooth hip. He still had his gun in his right. "Wait."

He walked to the bedpost and holstered the gun, then turned to look at her again. By this time, she had slithered onto the bed.

"Get those clothes off, Mister," she said. "We don't have all night."

He undressed and, naked, joined her on the bed. He wondered briefly if this was even fair to Maggie, but then he did sleep with her back in Big Fork. So this was only fair.

He took her in his arms and kissed her. She kissed him back with desperation, wrapped her arms and legs around him. Her skin was as smooth and hot as he remembered.

"Oh my God," she said, "I forgot how good you feel."

"I didn't forget anything about you," he said. "How you feel, how you smell . . ."

"How do I smell?" she asked, pressing her lips to his neck. "Tell me."

"You smell special."

"How?"

"Down there," he said, sliding his hand between her legs and stroking her. "All women smell good down there. Some sweet, some sour, but all good. But you . . .

"Me?"

He moved his fingers and she moaned.

"When you get very, very wet down there," he said, "you smell . . . intoxicating."

She giggled.

"Is that why you spent so much time down there?" she asked.

"Exactly," he said. "That's why I'm going to spend time down there right . . . now!"

He proceeded to kiss his way down her body until his face was nestled in her crotch. She was wet, but she would get wetter still, and that intoxicating aroma she secreted would fill his nostrils while he lapped her up with his tongue.

"Oh God," she said, reaching down to hold his head.

And there it was. He pressed his face to her and inhaled the dizzying scent of her. All the women he had ever been with had their own fragrance, and they all affected him. His cock felt engorged, as if it was going to explode. He wanted to stay there all night but didn't want to find out what would happen if Maggie woke up and came looking for Amy.

So he pulled his face away from her, slid up onto her, and drove his hard penis into her soaking wet pussy . . .

Chapter Twenty

Amy got out of Clint's bed before morning, assuring him that Maggie would never know.

"Good," he said, "I don't want to start any trouble between you two."

She kissed him and slipped into the hall, leaving behind that heady scent of hers.

In the morning, he rose and tried to wash that aroma off without taking a full bath. He used most of the water in the pitcher-and-basin on the dresser, and plenty of soap, then went down to have breakfast with the two women.

Maggie and Amy were already seated and drinking coffee when he arrived.

"Did you sleep well?" Amy asked him. Nothing in her tone or expression betrayed a thing.

"I slept really well," he said. "You two?"

"Like a log," Amy said.

"Like the dead," Maggie said. "I'd say I'm very well rested today."

"I'm going to get as much information as I can from Nell today, about the phony me, and then go looking," Clint said. "What will you two be doing?"

"We discussed it," Maggie said, "and decided to stay and support Nell, especially if you do manage to bring the man back here."

"We wanna give her strength," Amy said, "which I don't think she'll be gettin' from her parents."

Clint had to agree with that, especially when it came to Noble Livingston. The man didn't seem to have any sympathy for his daughter and seemed to feel that he was the aggrieved party.

Since they wanted to support Nell, Maggie and Amy walked with Clint to the livery where he saddled Eclipse while the hostler saddled the horses for the ladies.

During the ride out to the house, Maggie asked, "Any chance I could come with you when you go looking for him?"

"No," he said. "I have no idea who this fella is, what he's like with a gun. I have to be able to focus when I catch up to him and having you along would be too distracting."

"Distracting in what way?" Amy asked.

"Not the way you're thinking," Clint said. "I mean I'd be worried she might get hurt."

"I can take care of myself," Maggie told him.

"With a gun?"

"Well, no, but—"

"Then the answer is still no."

They rode the rest of the way in silence.

***

During breakfast in the Livingston house, Noble told his daughter, "When that Clint Adams gets here, you tell him everythin' he needs to know to catch the varmint who soiled you. Understand?"

"Yes, Papa."

"Don't try to protect him," her mother said. "He needs to pay for what he done."

"Yes, Mama."

"And see if you can convince Adams to bring the fella back here," Noble said. "I wanna kill 'im myself for what he done to us."

Nell looked at her father, wishing she could tell him that nothing had been done to him, it had been done to *her*. But she didn't have the nerve. So in the end she just said, "Yes, Papa."

***

Clint, Maggie and Amy reined in their horses in front of the house and dismounted.

"This must've been a nice house at one time," Maggie said.

"I offered to do some work around here," Clint said, "but now I'm having second thoughts."

"Why?" Amy asked. "It sure needs it."

"Now I'm thinking when I find this fella, I'll bring him back here and let him do all the work."

"That sounds like a good idea," Maggie said.

"The only problem is," Clint said, "I'd have to keep Noble from killing him first."

The front door of the house opened before they reached it and Nell stepped out.

"I'm ready, Mr. Adams," she said. "Can we walk and talk?"

"Whatever makes you more comfortable, Nell," he said.

Nell smiled at her two friends, then started walking away from the house with Clint.

"I thought I'd take you to the spot where I met Cli— him," Nell said, "and then start tellin' you what you wanna know."

"Another good idea," Clint said. "I'm glad you've been giving this some thought, Nell."

"I want to make sure I get it all straight," she said, "And give you a real chance at catching up to him."

"Just tell me everything you remember, Nell," Clint said. "That should do it."

Chapter Twenty-One

"It was here," she said, when they reached a small water hole.

"What were you doing?" he asked.

"I was taking a bath," she said. "When I realized he was standin' here watchin' me, I froze."

"And what did he do?"

"He was real nice," she said. "He said he was sorry, and then turned his back so I could get out and get dressed."

"What else did he say?"

"That I was too pretty not to watch." She ducked her head shyly.

"It sounds like he knew the right things to say," Clint commented. "Did he introduce himself?"

"Not that time," she said. "We—we arranged to meet here again the next day. That was when he told me his name was Clint Adams."

"And knowing the reputation behind that name," he asked, "it didn't occur to you that he was too young?"

She hesitated, then said, "I think I just wanted to believe him."

"I can understand that," Clint said.

"You can?" she asked, looking surprised.

"Let's sit," he said, as they came to a couple of likely looking boulders. "Tell me what you two talked about?"

"Everythin'?" she asked.

"Yes," he said, "I'm hoping he might have told you something that would give me a clue to where he went."

"Well," she said, "we talked for a week before he—before we—I mean, until he left."

"Just start from the beginning," he said.

"The bath?"

"Sure," he said, "start from your bath."

***

Clint listened to everything Nell had to say about her "Clint Adams," and only interrupted her a couple of times to ask a question. Then, when she was finished talking, he took a few moments to absorb everything.

"Was any of that helpful?" she asked.

"I'm sure it will be," he said, "but just let me ask a few more questions."

"All right," she said. "I'll do my best to answer them."

"First, I need to know what he looks like," Clint said, "exactly, and then we'll take it from there."

After she described the man physically, Clint asked, "Did he give you any idea where he came here from? Or where he lived?"

"He didn't talk about himself all that much," she admitted. "He mostly said nice things to me, things I'd never heard from anyone else, before."

Clint wondered how many other girls this man had tricked, and if he was the only one the man had ever impersonated.

"Let's walk back," he suggested, helping her to her feet.

As they walked, he studied her profile. She was a pretty girl who, in a few years, would probably be a stunner. Of course, that would only happen if she could avoid the hard work that had taken its toll on her mother, who was probably in her forties, but looked much older.

"There is one thing I remember," Nell said, as they approached the house.

"What's that?"

"He really seemed to know his way around this area," she said. "He took me to a couple of places for picnics and . . . that was when we had sex. He seemed to know that no one would ever find us there."

"Okay, that's good," he said. "If he knows the area, he may be from here. Or, at least, he spent a lot of time here."

"Then maybe he has friends," she said.

"That's what I'm going to find out," Clint told her. "And while I'm doing that, I'll need you to stay here with your mother and father."

"But when you find him, you'll bring him to me, right?" Nell asked.

"Will you have something to say to him?" Clint asked.

"I'll have a lot to say," she replied, strongly. "He made a fool of me, and he's gonna pay."

"Okay, then," Clint said, "you just stay here so that when I get him, I won't have to go looking for you."

"Don't worry," she said, as they approached the house, "I'll be here."

***

When Clint rode back to town, Maggie and Amy accompanied him.

"Was she helpful?" Maggie asked.

"Very. And I think she's finally at the point where she's going to show some moxie."

"Good," Amy said, "maybe she'll also have something, to say to her father."

"That's a family thing I'm not going to get involved in," Clint said. "My only goal is to find this phony Clint Adams."

Chapter Twenty-Two

Sheriff Brett looked up from his desk as his office door opened and Clint Adams walked in. He leaned back and tried to control his heartbeat. For all he knew, the Gunsmith could hear men's hearts. The man *was* a goddamned legend.

"Mr. Adams," he said, "what can I do for you?"

"I'm looking for somebody, Sheriff."

"For what reason?" Brett asked. "Not to kill him, I hope."

"That's not my intention," Clint said.

"Then what is your intention?"

"Since there's a man going around telling people he's me," Clint said, "I think I should find him and stop him."

"Yeah, you mentioned that," Brett said. "What can I do?"

"I've managed to get a description," Clint said. "I thought maybe you'd recognize him."

"I'm listening."

"Tall, late twenties, maybe thirty, handsome, smooth-skinned, like he doesn't have to shave often, blue eyes and a, uh, pleasant smile."

"Sounds like a real miscreant," Brett said. "I prefer my bad guys mean lookin'."

"Does that description match anyone you know, or you've seen in town?"

"No, it doesn't," Brett said.

"All right, then," Clint said, "I just want you to know I'll be looking around, asking questions, trying to find somebody who does know him."

"That's fine," Brett said. "As long as you don't kill anybody, you can do whatever you want. Just keep me informed, all right?"

"Agreed," Clint said, turned and left.

Brett put his face in his hands for a few seconds, then rubbed vigorously. Adams had the description of his brother down pat. All they shared were the blue eyes—their mother's eyes. The sheriff's father was a brutish, ugly man, while Simon's father was handsome. Apparently, their mother didn't have a certain type.

He stood up, took his hat off a wall hook. He had to find out if Simon had done what he was told and left town.

***

Clint left the sheriff's office and headed for the nearest saloon. It was a small town, but even small ones tended to have more than one place to drink.

The first one was called The Last Bullet Saloon. He ordered a beer and gave the bartender the description of the man he was looking for.

"You're askin' the wrong person," the bartender said.

"Do you know the man I should ask, then?"

"No, no," the middle-aged bartender said, "I mean with a description like that, you shouldn't be askin' a man, you should be askin' a woman."

"That's a very good point," Clint said, looking around. "When do your saloon girls come on?"

"In a few hours," the bartender said. "Or you could go to the cathouse and ask there."

"This little town has a cathouse?"

"And three saloons," the bartender said. "Folks hereabouts like their pleasures."

"All the saloons have girls?"

"Yeah, they do. We have the best lookin' ones, though," the bartender said. "Make sure you come back and have a look."

"The cathouse," Clint said. "Where is it?"

***

The cathouse was at the north end of town—why were they always at the north end or south end, and never right in the center? In any case, this one was called Lady George's Palace of Pleasures.

The wooden front door was covered with peeling pink paint. He tried it, found it locked and knocked. Some bordellos stayed open all day, some kept certain hours.

The door opened and a vapid looking blonde peered out at him while shielding her eyes from the sun.

"What the hell," she said. "We ain't open."

"I know," he said, "but I'm not looking for company, I'm looking for information."

"Come back when we're open," she said, and started to close the door.

"I'm afraid I need answers now," he said, putting his foot in the door.

She glared at him.

"Then you're gonna wanna talk to the boss," she told him. "Wait here."

She tried to close the door again, but he kept his foot in place. She turned and walked away. There were no sounds from inside. The place was quiet as a tomb, at the moment.

But he knew that wouldn't last. Sure as hell, not in a place like this.

Chapter Twenty-Three

The girl returned, holding her ratty robe closed and looking annoyed.

"Follow me," she said. She led him to a door and pointed. "That's George's office."

She left him standing there, so he assumed he was to go in. He opened the door and entered, expecting to find a "Lady" George. Instead, he found a big, florid-faced man in his fifties seated behind a desk. Clint assumed this was George.

"You're lucky I'm awake and doin' some paper-work," the man said around a thick cigar stuck right in the middle of his face. "Whataya want? And who the hell are ya?"

"My name's Clint Adams."

It didn't take long for that to sink in. The man ignored his paperwork and looked up at Clint.

"You gonna shoot up my joint?"

"That's not my plan."

"What *is* your plan?" George said.

"I'm looking for someone," Clint said. "I was hoping one of your girls would recognize his description and tell me where I can find him."

"You gonna kill 'im?"

"No."

"Well, we got no customers in the place now," George said, standing up. "Let me get the girls together for you in the sittin' room and you can check with them all."

"I appreciate that."

"I ain't about to tell the Gunsmith he can't have what he wants," George said, "I ain't that brave. Wait here a minute."

George left the room, and Clint decided to have a look at the papers on the desk. On one of them he saw the name George Callaghan. He wondered if the man was being so cooperative simply because he was afraid. As it turned out, that wasn't the case. When the door reopened, George stepped in and three men with guns came in behind him.

"I don't know who you think you're foolin', Adams," George said. "Whoever sent you, tell 'em I ain't afraid."

The three men had guns in their hands. The situation could have gone badly very fast.

"Just take it easy, George," he said. "Nobody sent me."

"Yeah, right," George said, "you're here lookin' for some man. Get 'im out of here, boys. And Dent, if you wanna fill 'im full of lead, wait until you're outside."

"Right, boss," one of the men said.

"You're making a mistake, George."

"I don't make mistakes, Adams."

"Let's go," Dent said, waving his gun, "and do us a favor, go for your gun."

Clint didn't see any reason to do that. These three men were just doing their jobs.

"George Callaghan, right?" Clint asked.

"That's my name."

"Good," Clint said. "I want to remember."

He allowed the three men to walk him out of the building. When they got outside, Dent couldn't resist.

"So whataya say, Adams?" he asked. "You gonna go for that gun?"

"Sure," he said, "the three of you just holster yours and let's see what happens."

The two men standing just behind Dent fidgeted and exchanged a look.

"Dent . . ." one of them said, warningly.

"Yeah, yeah," Dent said. Clint could see he was tempted, but he also knew the other two men wouldn't back his play. "Some other time, Adams."

"Dent," Clint said. "I'll remember that, too."

Clint decided to walk away and maybe come back another time.

***

He went back to the Last Bullet and ordered a beer.

"You finished at the whorehouse?" the man asked.

"Didn't get very far," Clint said. "Lady George had his bouncers walk me out."

"Dent," the bartender said, nodding. "He's a mean one."

"What about Callaghan?"

"I guess I shoulda warned you," the bartender said. "He thinks everybody is out to get him."

"Yeah, that's the way he acted," Clint said. "He was pretty sure somebody had sent me there."

"Well," the bartender said, "you wanna wait a while, my girls should start comin' down pretty soon."

"This your place?" Clint asked.

"No, but I manage it, so I call 'em my girls," he said. "It's the only way an ugly lug like me is gonna be able to say that."

Clint couldn't argue, because the bartender was pretty ugly.

"I'll take another beer."

Chapter Twenty-Four

When the saloon girls came down the stairs, the men started to cheer. Clint saw a blonde, a brunette and a redhead, all in their twenties, all very pretty.

"I told you," the bartender said. "Best girls in town."

"I'll have to see the others before I agree," Clint said, "but they *are* pretty little things, aren't they?"

"Now you can go ahead and ask them your questions," the man said, "but do me a favor and do it one at a time, all right?"

"Agreed."

The girls were Trixie, Belle and Diana. He doubted they were real names, but that didn't matter. He described the phony "Clint Adams" to them, but none of the three recognized him.

"But that's odd," Trixie, the blonde, said. She was the last one he talked with.

"What do you mean?"

"If he's as handsome and charming as you say," she replied, "why wouldn't he come into a saloon? There's only one reason I can think of."

"And that is?"

"He didn't want to be seen," she said. "At least, not in town."

"Good point, Trixie," he said. "Thank you."

She gave him a coy look and asked, "Is there anything else I can do for you?"

"I'm sure there is," he said, "but not tonight. Thanks, again."

Clint went back to the bar.

"Any luck?" the man asked.

"Yes, and no," Clint said. "What's your name?"

"They call me Bub."

"Well, thanks, Bub," Clint said. "I'm going to go check those other saloons now."

"The Yellow Lady, and Declan's Saloon," Bub said.

"Do they have what it would take to attract a young cowboy?" Clint asked.

"They have what we have," Bub said, "but on a smaller, cheaper scale. That includes the girls."

"Well, once I've been there, I'll be able to decide for myself," Clint said.

"Good," Bub said. "Let me know when you do."

"'night, Bub."

"Yeah, see ya . . ."

***

Clint went to the Yellow Lady first. Over the bar was the painting of a lady in a yellow dress, with a yellow rose in her hair.

"Yeah," the bartender said, looking up at the painting, "it makes more sense than 'The Last Bullet.'"

"Why?" Clint asked. "Just because there are no bullets inside?"

"Hey," the bartender said, pointing to the lady, "this is classy."

Clint looked around. The interior was also somebody's idea of classy, but the fact was it was too bright and obvious for that.

"Do you own the place?" Clint asked.

"I do," the man said. "My name's Frank Maxwell. Who're you?"

"Clint Adams. I just need to talk to your ladies."

"What's the Gunsmith need with my girls?"

"Information. Do you mind?"

"No, not at all," Maxwell said. "As long as they go back to work after you talk to them."

"I'll do my best to not interfere with their work," Clint said. "I just need to describe somebody to them and see if they know who he is."

"Well, go ahead," Maxwell said, waving his hand. "There they are."

Clint looked around, saw two girls working the floor. The Yellow Lady was only half full, so he'd have no problem isolating each girl for a few moments.

Their dresses were gaudy and their make-up garish. Obviously, this was what Maxwell thought of as class.

"I'll have a beer," Clint said.

"Comin' up."

Clint accepted the mug, said, "Thanks," and then carried it to the far end of the bar, where one of the girls stood.

"Hello, there," she said. "I'm Wanda."

Wanda was in her thirties, and actually pretty underneath all the make-up. Her voluptuous breasts were almost being pushed out of her dress.

"Hello, Wanda," Clint said. "Your boss says I can ask you some questions."

"That right? About what?"

"A man I'm looking for," Clint said. "I just want to know if you've seen him."

"What's his name?"

"I don't have a name, just a description." Clint gave it to her while she leaned an elbow on the bar and listened.

"Could be a lot of men," she said, when he was done. "We get plenty of customers in here."

"This one apparently always has a pleasant smile on his face," he said.

"Then I ain't seen 'im," she said. "Most of the losers who come in here only have evil smiles, or angry frowns."

"And why would that be?"

"Oh, that's easy," she said. "They hate this town."

"Ah."

"Did you wanna ask Annie about his guy?" she said, pointing to the blonde saloon girl.

"Do you think she might know him?"

"Maybe," Wanda said, "she knows a lot of men. I'll get 'er for you."

Wanda went over to Annie, spoke to her briefly, then the dark-haired girl came over to Clint. She was younger, not as garishly made-up. She was pretty enough not to need so much of it.

"Wanda says you gotta ask me somethin', Mister," Annie said. "If you're lookin' for a poke, you should go to the cathouse, not here. I ain't no whore."

"I'm not looking for a poke, Annie," he said, "I just have a question."

"That's all right, then."

Clint described the man he was looking for, and Annie listened intently.

"I dunno," she said, "we see lots of men in here. But a pleasant smile? Not many of those. Most of these men, their smiles ain't so pleasant. I'm sorry, Mister, I don't think I seen 'im."

"Thanks, anyway."

Clint left the Yellow Lady, wondering if he should even bother heading over to Declan's Saloon. It seemed like this fella may have been staying out of sight, except for seeing Nell Livingston.

Chapter Twenty-Five

Sheriff Brett entered Declan's Saloon, spotted his brother Simon at a back table and stormed over to him.

"Are you crazy?" he asked.

"What?" Simon looked up, a blank look on his face.

"Clint Adams is out lookin' for you."

"What, now?"

"Yeah, right now," Brett said, grabbing the younger man and yanking him out of his chair. "He's checkin' saloons and he'll be here any minute."

"Well, so what?" Simon said. "I can take 'im, Dan. I can!"

"Don't be a fool," Sheriff Brett said. "He's the goddamn Gunsmith!"

"I wanna face 'im!"

"Not in my town!" Sheriff Brett snapped. "We just found out we're brothers. I don't wanna watch you get shot, already."

"We could do it together, then," Simon said. "The Brett Brothers against the Gunsmith."

"Just stay alive long enough for me to think about it. That's all I ask."

"Sure, Dan," Simon said, "sure, I can do that."

"Then get out of here and lay low," the sheriff told him.

Simon grabbed his brother's arm and said, "Promise me *you* won't try to take 'im yourself."

"I promise," Sheriff Brett said. "If we do it, we'll do it together."

Simon started for the front door.

"Go out the back!" Dan yelled.

***

When Clint entered Declan's Saloon, he was surprised to find Sheriff Brett having a drink at the bar.

"Out making rounds, Sheriff?" he asked, sidling up alongside the lawman.

"Oh, Adams," Brett said, looking surprised. "Yeah, as a matter of fact, I am. Buy you a beer?"

"Sure, why not?"

"Any luck findin' your man?"

"Not so far," Clint said, accepting the beer from the barkeep. "Nobody seems to remember a man with a pleasant smile. I never thought that'd be the sticking point. Seems the men around here aren't so pleasant."

"I'd have to agree with that," Sheriff Brett said. "Just look around at the sour faces in here. Most of these yahoos wish they were somewhere else."

"What about you, Sheriff?" Clint asked. "You wish you were somewhere else?"

"Every day," Brett said, "but it's too late for me. This is my last stop, when it comes to wearin' a badge."

"You been sprouting tin a long time, then?"

"Thirty years or more," Brett said. "In more towns than I care to remember."

Clint looked around, commented, "No girls in here?"

"Nope," Brett said, "just whiskey and beer."

"Might account for the sour faces," Clint said. He looked at the bartender, a man in his forties who gave him a sour look.

Brett laughed and said, "You might be right about that. You gonna try the whorehouse again?"

"I don't think 'Lady' George would like that so much," Clint said.

"Well," Brett said, "you might find some of the girls out during the day, shoppin' or havin' lunch."

"How will I know them?" Clint asked.

"By the looks the decent women in town'll be tossin' their way," Brett said.

"And how will I know who the decent women are?"

"By the sour looks on *their* faces," Brett told him.

Clint finished his beer and said, "Thanks for the drink, Sheriff, and the tip."

As Clint Adams left Declan's, the Sheriff breathed a sigh of relief.

Chapter Twenty-Six

Clint spent the rest of the evening in his room with Robin Hood. He was getting into the story and enjoying characters like Little John and Friar Tuck.

In the morning he ate breakfast in the small dining room of his hotel, where it seemed the desk clerk was also the waiter.

"You're not the cook, too, are you?" Clint asked the young man.

"No sir," the boy said, "but I hope to be, one day."

Clint looked around at the other diners. He assumed they were all from out of town, since there didn't seem to be a sour look among them. They had the good fortune of knowing they would be leaving this town, and soon.

On the other hand, the desk clerk/waiter didn't seem to be sour at all. But Clint could've put that down to his young age.

He decided not to tax the cook's abilities and simply ordered ham-and-eggs and coffee. The coffee turned out to be weak, the eggs runny, and the ham paper thin. He was sure the boy could've done better when only half trying.

"Can I ask you something?" he said to the waiter when he came for his plate.

"Yessir," the clerk said, "there are better places to eat in town. I can tell ya a couple."

"I was going to ask you about a man I'm looking for," Clint said, and gave the youngster the description he had.

"Fella like that wouldn't be stayin' here, sir."

"I'm staying here," Clint pointed out.

"I figure you got to town and didn't know no better," the waiter said.

"You've got a point," Clint said. "Why don't you tell me about those other places to eat . . ."

***

Clint decided, upon leaving the hotel, to keep his eyes open for the prostitutes who might be out shopping or having lunch. He saw that the sheriff was right about the decent women in town. They seemed as grumpy and unhappy as the men. As he passed them and touched the brim of his hat, they seemed to become even grumpier. The small town malaise was affecting all of the denizens of Collinsville.

It wouldn't be hard to spot women who were shop-ping, as it seemed they only had the mercantile to patronize. He took up a position across the street and prepared to wait.

It didn't take long.

Three girls came walking up to the mercantile just as two of the town's "decent" ladies came out. The two sour faced women thrust their noses into the air, and Clint quickly knew them from the whores.

The whores had better manners.

He crossed the street and entered the mercantile.

". . . we keep their husbands happy, so they don't bother them when they get home," one of the whores was saying. "They should be thankin' us."

One of the three whores was the tall, washed out blonde who had answered the door when Clint knocked. She was also the one complaining.

"I agree with you," he said.

All three girls turned and looked at him.

"You!" the washed-out blonde said.

"Me," Clint said. "I'm on your side. Those sour-faced battle-axes should be thanking you."

The other two girls giggled. They were younger than the blonde, who turned to them and shushed them.

"Go do your shoppin'," she said.

They scurried off while the blonde turned to Clint and asked, "Whataya want?"

"Just some questions."

"George says we shouldn't talk to you," the girl said.

"Do you let George tell you who you can talk to when you're out on your own?" Clint asked. "You strike me as a woman who had a mind of her own." Clint took some money from his pocket, catching the girl's eye. She turned and looked over her shoulder to see where the other two girls were, then snatched the money from Clint's hand.

"I guess it doesn't hurt to answer a question or two," she said, reasonably.

Clint quickly gave her the description of the man he was looking for, complete with his pleasant smile.

"If a man with a pleasant smile came into the house, I'd snatch 'im up," she told Clint. "We get creepy, leering, lewd smiles, ugly smiles," she told him. "That's about it."

"Thanks . . ."

"Velma," she said.

"Thanks, Velma."

"Thank you for the shoppin' money."

She turned to join her friends in their shopping.

Clint stepped outside, convinced that, if this man was in town, he was keeping a low profile—no drinking, no gambling and no whores.

What else was there?

Chapter Twenty-Seven

"What's that?" Ansel Happ asked

"It's a telegram, Pa," Festus Happ said. He had walked into the saloon and dropped something on his father's table.

"Yeah? From?"

"A place called Collinsville, Wyoming," Festus said. "Well, it's from a bigger town near Collinsville, because that town's too small to have—"

"What's it say, Festus?" Ansel asked.

"It's about the Gunsmith," Festus said. "He's in Collinsville."

Ansel grabbed the telegram, unfolded it and read it, then crumpled it in his hand.

"Go get everybody."

"Everybody?"

"Your brothers," Ansel said, "your cousins, your uncles . . . everybody. We're goin' to Collinsville."

***

"So you've found nothing?" Maggie asked.

They were seated, along with Amy, in a café the hotel desk clerk had told Clint would be a better place to eat.

"I've managed to find out that he doesn't want to be seen," Clint said, "otherwise why would he never have been in one of the saloons?"

"Did you try the whorehouse?" Maggie asked.

"I did," Clint said. "He wasn't seen there, either."

"This was last year," Amy said. "Could it be that people just don't remember him?"

"It's possible," Clint said, "except that the way Nell describes him—"

"Don't forget," Maggie said, "she was in love with him."

"That colors the way a girl sees a man," Amy said.

"So her description—"

"—might be exaggerated," Maggie finished.

He sat back in his chair, looked down at his half-eaten pork.

"You may have a point," he said. "No wonder nobody's recognizing him. He doesn't exist. Not in the way she saw him."

"So now what?" Maggie asked.

"I'm still looking for a stranger," Clint said. "His look may be exaggerated, but maybe his charm isn't."

"As far as a young girl is concerned," Maggie said.

"So her parents never saw this man?"

"Not that they've said."

"And Nell isn't that much help, after all," Clint commented.

"Oh, she'd probably be able to point him out if she saw him," Amy said.

"She's just not describing him very well," Maggie said.

"If he only impersonated me to bed her," Clint said, "and he's not doing it anymore, he's going to be hard to find."

"He might decide to do it again," Maggie said, "to another girl. Could you live with that if you gave up searching for him?"

"I didn't say I was giving up," Clint said. "I'm just saying it's going to be harder and take longer."

"We can help," Maggie said, and Amy nodded.

"You should both leave," he said, "get on with your lives. There's something else I'm going to have to deal with sooner or later."

"What's that?"

"The man I killed before we left Big Fork," he said, "has a family. I've been told they won't take his death lightly."

"So they're going to come after you?" Amy asked.

"Probably."

"How many?" Maggie asked.

"I don't know," he said, "but I was told it was a big family."

"Then you'll need help," Maggie said.

"That may be."

"We should stay," Amy said.

"No."

"He thinks he'll be worried about us," Maggie said to Amy, "and get killed."

"It's true," he said, "I need to know the two of you are safe."

"So where should we go?" Amy asked.

"Anyplace but here," he said.

"For how long?"

He shrugged.

"Who knows? We have to get on with our lives," he told them.

Maggie and Amy looked at each other for a long moment. Something passed between them, but Clint Adams had no idea what it was.

"Ladies . . ."

"We'll go," Maggie said.

"But you better not get yourself killed," Amy warned him.

"Not getting myself killed," Clint said, "is always uppermost in my mind."

Chapter Twenty-Eight

The Happs entered the saloon. Ansel stood at the bar and watched as they filed in. Two of Uriah's brothers, six of his cousins, and two of his uncles.

"There are eleven of us," he said.

"Should be enough to take care of one fella," his older brother, Hector, said.

"But it's the Gunsmith," the younger brother, Levon, said.

Four of the cousins were Hector's boys, while the other two were Levon's.

"I think we can do it, Pa," one of Hector's sons said. "I mean, come on, one man—even the Gunsmith—he can't beat eleven of us."

Patriarch Ansel looked at his sons, nephews and brothers, then finished his beer and said, "All right, then. Let's go."

They all went outside, where their horses were saddled and waiting.

As they mounted up, Ansel turned his horse so he could look at all of them.

"This is for Uriah!"

***

Clint walked Maggie and Amy to the livery and saddled their horses for them, then walked them outside.

"Where should we go?" Amy asked, again.

"Just ride," he said, holding the horses while they mounted. "Go wherever the road takes you."

"Is that what you do?" Maggie asked.

"It's what I did for years," he said. "Not so much, anymore."

The two women eyed each other after they had mounted. Clint knew they both wanted to stay with him, but Maggie had been right. Having them here would most likely get him killed when he ran up against the Happ family.

"Ride out, now," Clint said.

"Will we ever see you again?" Amy asked.

"Who knows?"

Sadly, both women turned their horses and rode away.

***

Simon Brett heard someone in the water hole just up ahead. When he came within sight of it, he saw the female. He had hoped it would be a girl taking a bath, but it was a woman doing laundry.

He watched her for a short time. She appeared to be in her early twenties, somewhere between girl and woman. She was primed for him.

He came out of the brush, and she turned when she heard him.

"Hello," he said.

She didn't answer, seemed wary.

"Don't be afraid," he said. "I'm friendly."

He came closer. She had been kneeling at the water's edge, but now stood. He thought she was only seconds from running from him.

"Do you come here often?" he asked.

"Y-yes," she said. "To do laundry, and to . . . to . . ."

"Bathe?"

She blushed

"Yes."

She was pretty, with corn silk hair and a slim body underneath a thin, cotton dress. Because it had gotten somewhat wet while she was doing laundry, he could see the outline of her breasts and nipples.

"I won't bother you," he said. "You can keep doin' your laundry. I'll just watch."

She frowned.

"You want to watch me do laundry?"

"Sure."

"Why?"

"Well," he said, "I don't think I've ever seen anythin' as pretty."

She laughed and said, "You're funny."

And just like that, she relaxed . . .

***

He chatted with her as she washed the clothes, and he could see that there were men's things there—full grown men, and small males. Turned out she was washing her father and brother's clothes, as well as her own.

"What about your mother?" he asked.

"She died when I was a baby," she said. "I do all the washin' and cleanin' and cookin'. I take care of the family, even though I'm the youngest."

"That must make you real tired sometimes," he said.

"Yes, it does."

"Must not leave much time for your boyfriend," he said.

"Oh, I don't have a boyfriend."

"I can't believe a girl as pretty as you doesn't have a beau," he said. "What's your name?"

"Lisa," she said. "What's yours?"

"I'm Clint," he said, "Clint Adams."

Chapter Twenty-Nine

With Maggie and Amy gone, Clint could give all of his thoughts to finding his impersonator. He decided to stop into the Last Bullet—he didn't think it was such a bad name for a saloon—and talk to Bub, the bartender.

***

Bub put a mug down in front of him and asked, "No luck, huh?"

"Turns out I might be looking for somebody who doesn't even exist," Clint said.

"Howzat?"

Clint told him how the description had come from a young girl.

"Oh, I getcha," Bub said. "What she saw ain't exactly what was there."

"Right.

"So whataya gonna do now?"

"I'm not sure. I don't have much of a description to go on. Tall, young, charming."

"And all that about his smile?" Bub asked. "His look?"

"In the eyes of a young girl," Clint said.

"I don't envy you havin' to figure out what this guy really looks like," Bub said.

"This was last year," Clint said, "roughly about this time. Do you remember any strangers from then?"

Bub gave it some thought, then shook his head.

"If there were strangers here then, I'd remember," he said. "This is a small town and we don't get that many visitors who stay for more than a drink, or a stop at the mercantile. Or the whorehouse."

"The whorehouse," Clint repeated. "That sounds like it'd be my best bet, but George Callaghan is not being very cooperative."

"I suppose you met Dent?"

"I did."

"He might be your best bet," Bub said.

"You think he'd talk to me?"

Bub shrugged.

"If he's not around Callaghan, Dent's not a bad guy. You buy him a drink, and that might be all it takes."

"Does he drink here?"

"On occasion," Bub said. "But I think he pretty much uses all three saloons in town equally. You'd just have to see which one you find him in."

Clint looked around.

"Well, he's not here," he said, "so I might as well look in the other two."

"Finish your beer first," Bub said. "You won't get beer this good over there."

Clint did as Bub suggested and emptied his mug before leaving.

***

Dent didn't like drinking at Lady George's. He was never able to finish one drink before somebody needed to be taught a lesson. So he took his drinks in the saloons and sat alone when he did. And never the same saloon two days in a row.

He sat quietly, working on a cold mug of beer in Declan's Saloon. There were only a few other patrons around him, and the sour looking bartender behind the bar. He wasn't bothered by the fact that there were no saloon girls. He had enough of the girls in the whorehouse. Time without their company and chatter was a blessing.

He was working on his second beer when the front door opened—Declan's didn't have batwing doors—and a man he recognized came in. He'd seen him at the whorehouse, when George had him show him the way out.

Clint Goddamn Adams.

***

Clint had checked The Yellow Lady and had not found Dent there. That left him with Declan's Saloon, although he wondered why anyone would want to drink there.

When he walked in, Dent was easy to spot since he was one of only a few customers, and was seated alone at a table.

"Beer?" the bartender called out to him.

"No, that's all right," Clint said, waving a hand.

"Either drink," the dour looking man said, "or leave."

"Fine," Clint said, approaching the bar, "then give me a beer."

"Comin' up."

He quickly set a mug on the bar. Clint picked it up, noticed that it wasn't very cold. Also, the glass wasn't all that clean.

"Thanks."

Clint carried the beer over to Dent's table. The bouncer looked up at him.

"Can I help you?"

"You mind if I sit down?" Clint asked.

"We're not in the whorehouse," Dent said, "so I can't throw you out, can I?"

"I'll take that as a yes," Clint said, and sat.

Chapter Thirty

"What's on your mind?" Dent asked.

"Strangers."

"There are a lot of those."

"I'm actually looking for one particular stranger."

"Wasn't that what you were talkin' to my boss about?" Dent asked.

"Yes," Clint said, "but at the time I had the wrong description."

"So whataya got now?" Dent asked.

"Actually, less than before," Clint said, "but since you're not one of the people I talked to . . . about a year ago, do you remember any strangers at the whorehouse?"

"Probably."

"Probably?"

"We do get strangers as customers, even though most of them come from this and adjoining counties."

"Seems to me, with that many regulars, strangers would stand out."

"You might be right."

"Then do me a favor and think back," Clint said. "How many strangers?"

"I don't know for sure I can tell you that, Adams," Dent said.

"You mean your boss, Callaghan, wouldn't like it?"

"He wouldn't," Dent said, "but that's not what I mean. I think the girls would be able to tell us better than I could."

"Us?"

"Well, you want my help, right?"

"Yes," Clint said, "but I didn't think you'd be offering it so willingly."

"My boss doesn't like you," Dent said.

"I figured that."

"That's a good enough reason for me to help you," Dent said. "See, I don't like him."

"Then why do you work for him?"

"He pays me well," Dent said. "And besides, who really likes their boss?"

"So you'll talk to the girls?"

"Sure," Dent said. "But you'll have to give me what you've got."

"I think we can assume he's tall, not old, and charming," Clint said.

"I'll see if I can make that work."

"Can we meet here tomorrow night?" Clint asked.

"Sure," Dent said. "I don't know if I'll get to talk to all the girls by then, but some."

"I appreciate this, Dent."

"What do you need this guy for?"

"He's been telling some people that he's me," Clint said. "I want to stop him."

"That's good," Dent said, standing up. "Maybe he told that to one of the girls."

"That'd be too much to hope for," Clint said.

"Well, we'll find out," Dent said. "Look, instead of meeting here tomorrow night, meet me at the Yellow Lady. I don't like drinkin' at the same place two nights in a row."

"I'll see you there."

Dent left the saloon, and Clint carried his warm beer in a dirty glass back to the bar.

"How'd you do that?" the barman asked.

"Do what?"

"Get Dent to help you," the man said. "He don't help nobody. In fact, he don't even usually talk to nobody."

"I guess I just found the right way to approach him," Clint said, putting the beer down on the bar and pushing it toward the bartender. "Try cleaning that glass next time, before you serve it to somebody."

"Yeah," the bartender said, "right."

***

Sheriff Brett checked all three saloons and didn't see his brother in any of them. He doubted that he'd left the area, but at least he was keeping out of sight.

The kid was a rascal when it came to girls, there was no doubt about that. But that wasn't something Simon Brett thought he should die for. As far as using the Gunsmith's name, that was just stupid. Dan Brett hoped the talking to he'd given to Simon would cure him of that habit. How stupid could you be to claim you were the deadliest gun the West had ever known? You had to know at some point someone was going to step up and try to make you prove it.

As Sheriff Brett peered through the grimy window of Declan's Saloon to check for his brother, he saw Clint Adams sitting with Dent, the bouncer from the whorehouse. Simon had sworn to him he'd never been to the cathouse, but in the short time he'd known his half-brother, he knew him to be a habitual liar. Hopefully, if Simon *had* ever visited Lady George's, he hadn't done it under the name Clint Adams—or his real name.

He withdrew before either man left the saloon.

Chapter Thirty-One

After both Clint Adams and Dent left Declan's, Sheriff Brett had gone in and talked with the bartender. That was the reason he now knew that Clint Adams was discounting a large part of Nell Livingston's description of his brother. Brett knew for a fact that back when Simon had first ridden into town, there were no other strangers present. All Adams needed to do was find one person who remembered that. That person just might be a whore.

***

The next morning Clint had breakfast alone. Without Maggie and Amy there to chew on his ear, he had time to give his actions some thought. If this was simply the case of a woman accusing him of fathering her baby, he wouldn't even be there. But having someone claiming to be him wasn't something he could ignore. Of course, if the imposter happened to get himself killed, it might take some pressure off him for a while. He'd often wondered what his life might be like if everyone thought he was dead.

***

Brett decided the next morning to go over and have a talk with George Callaghan. He knocked on the faded, peeling door, and Velma, the tall blonde, opened it.

"Sheriff," she said, not concealing her surprise. She could count on the fingers of one hand the times the lawman had come to the whorehouse. "What can we do for ya?"

"I need to talk to George," Brett said.

"I'll tell him you're—"

"That's all right," Brett said, brushing past her. "I'll announce myself."

He walked through the interior to George's office door and entered without knocking. There was a naked girl sitting on the man's lap, bouncing up and down, big tits flopping about in his face.

"Tryin' out a new girl, George?" Brett asked.

"Jesus!" George said, looking over at the lawman. "What the hell, Brett—"

"We need to talk," the sheriff said. "You can finish tryin' the new girl out later."

The girl got off George's lap and tried to cover herself with her dress. She was young with lots of pale skin, most of it tits and butt.

134

"You're hired, sweetie," George said, adjusting his trousers. "Go and tell Velma I said to give you a room."

"Yes, sir," the girl said, and ran past Brett, who closed the door behind her.

"There's a lot of meat, there," the lawman said.

"Some men like that," George said. "I gotta keep my stock ready for any request." The man straightened his chair and leaned on his desk. "What's on your mind, Sheriff?"

"My brother."

"The kid? What'd he do now?"

"Still pretendin' to be the Gunsmith."

George sat back and laughed.

"What the hell is wrong with him?"

"He's young."

"But he ain't a kid," George said. "He's in his twenties. When's he gonna grow up?"

"Look, George," Brett said, "was he here last year? Or any time since?"

"You said you didn't want me lettin' him in," George reminded the lawman.

"Yeah, but maybe you did, just once," Brett said.

George fidgeted.

"Come on . . ." Brett said.

"He was here one time," George said, "spent some time with Lizzie."

"Does she still work here?"

"She does, but my girls have orders not to talk about their customers."

"Okay," Brett said, "this place and the Last Bullet are really the only two going concerns this town has. You want to keep it that way, right?"

George sighed.

"What do you want me to do?"

"I saw your man Dent in Declan's last night, with Clint Adams."

"Dent doesn't drink with anybody," George said.

"Well, he was drinkin' with the Gunsmith," Brett said. "I don't want him tellin' Adams that Simon was here."

"I'll talk to Dent," George said.

"Can you handle 'im?"

"I pay him," George said. "That means I can handle him."

"And the girl?" Brett asked. "Lizzie?"

"I'll talk to her, too," George said, "but it seems to me you better straighten your brother out."

"I'm tryin'," Brett said. "He's had a lot of years with no direction. I've only had one year to work on him."

"You'd think Adams being here looking for him would scare him," George said.

"I think he's too stupid to be scared," Brett said.

"'Stupid' can get you killed faster than anything else," George said. "Maybe you need to get Adams out of town."

"Believe me," Brett said, "I'm workin' on that, too."

Chapter Thirty-Two

Clint didn't like the idea of depending on Dent's dislike of his boss to get him some information. He was still going to have to do something himself. When he came out of the café after finishing his breakfast, he saw Sheriff Brett across the street. The lawman spotted him and crossed over, and he wondered if the lawman had been waiting for him?

"Adams," Brett said.

"You following me, Sheriff?"

"Not at all," the lawman assured him. "Just saw you from across the street, thought we'd have a walk."

"Anywhere in particular?"

"No."

As they started, Clint asked, "Any subject in particular?"

"Your reasons for bein' here," Brett said.

"I told you that," Clint said. "I'm looking for someone."

"And when you find him?"

"Like I said, I'm not here to kill anyone."

"Then what will you do when you catch . . . this man?" Brett asked.

"Teach him a lesson."

"How?"

"I'll know that when I find him," Clint said. "But for one thing, there's a girl he's wronged, and her family wants . . . justice."

"That's all?"

"For a start."

"So what are your plans, movin' forward?" Brett asked.

"I figure I've just got to keep asking questions."

"Here?" Brett asked. "In Collinsville? Don't you think it's possible he moved on?"

"It's possible, yes," Clint said. "But there's one thing Nell told me that's keeping me here."

"And what's that?"

"She said he seemed to know his way around," Clint explained. "As if he lived here."

"Ah," Brett said. "So you'll keep lookin'."

"Until I find out something that sends me elsewhere," Clint said.

"What about just . . . givin' it up?" Brett asked. "Maybe he's through impersonatin' you."

"I'm afraid I'd have to make sure of that, Sheriff," Clint said.

"Yes, well . . ." Brett stopped. "I suppose I can understand that. So you'll be around town a while longer."

"I'm afraid so."

"Well then," Brett said, "I guess I'll be seein' you around."

Brett turned and walked back the way they had come. Clint frowned, wondered what the lawman was really trying to find out, and continued walking.

***

It was obvious to Sheriff Dan Brett that he was going to have to get his brother to leave town, and the county. He just hoped Simon wouldn't do anything stupid before he could get to him.

***

Simon saw Lisa at the waterhole again. This time she wasn't doing laundry, she was bathing.

He stopped and watched her from hiding as she washed her naked body, and at one point he was sure she knew he was there. She stretched her hands up over her head, which lifted her firm, young breasts, which were tipped with distended brown nipples. At that point, he decided to step out and allow her to see he was there.

When she did, she turned to face him, and didn't bother to hide her nudity. This girl's shyness was fading very quickly, which he put down to the effect of his charm.

"Are you comin' in?" she asked.

"Are you invitin' me?"

She smiled coyly and asked, "Don't I look like I'm invitin' you?"

She watched as he sat down and removed his boots, then stood and removed the rest of his clothes. He returned the favor and allowed her to stare at his nude form as he stretched for her. But what she was staring at was between his legs, and it was growing. He thought about touching it and making it harder, but then decided to leave that to her, if it was what she wanted.

He walked into the waterhole until it was up to his thighs, then dove in and swam towards her. She was standing where the water was almost up to her breasts. As he swam toward her, she pushed off and did a back-stroke to a deeper part of the waterhole. When he got there, they both treaded water and stared at each other.

"Well," he said, "I wonder what's next?"

Chapter Thirty-Three

Sheriff Brett had a small house just outside of town, which came with the job. He only spent time there when he was off duty, which wasn't often, because he had no deputies. He'd looked everywhere else he could think of for Simon, so he tried there.

"Where've you been?" he demanded, when he found his brother sitting on his sofa.

"Out and about."

"Not good enough," the sheriff said. "Where?"

"Visitin' a friend," Simon said. "Whattsa matter?"

"Clint Adams is still lookin' for you," the sheriff said, "and the real you, this time, not the you some young girl described to him."

"How does he think he's gonna do that?"

"Tell me," the lawman said, "how many times have you been to Lady George's whorehouse?"

"Just once," Simon said. "I don't usually need to use whores, but I stopped in there when I first got here, last year."

"That's not good," Sheriff Brett said. "I saw Adams talkin' to Dent."

"Who?"

"The bouncer from the whorehouse."

"I didn't get bounced."

"Is the girl you were with gonna remember you?" Brett asked.

"I hope so," Simon said, with a grin.

"No," the sheriff said, "You hope not! What name did you use?"

"Just Simon."

"No last name?"

"No."

"And you didn't say you were related to me?"

"No, brother," Simon said, "I wouldn't want to embarrass you."

"Look," the lawman said, "you need to get out of town."

"No."

"What?"

"This is my home, now," Simon said. "I'm not gonna let anybody run me out."

"Nobody's runnin' you out," the sheriff said. "Once I get rid of Adams, you can come back. Just stay in touch so I know where you are."

Simon frowned.

"How far do I have to go?"

"Not far," the lawman said. "Just leave town, get out of the county."

"Yes, all right," Simon said. "I'll leave tomorrow."

"And wherever you go," Dan Brett said to him, "don't use the name Clint Adams."

"What name should I use?"

"Not his," the lawman said, "and not your own. Any other name will do."

Simon frowned.

"I'll think of somethin' good."

"You know," Sheriff Brett said, sitting down next to his brother, "you still haven't given me a good reason for using the Gunsmith's name in the first place."

"He has a reputation with a gun," Simon said, "and with women. But I was only interested in using his reputation with women."

"How often have you used his name before you got here?" the sheriff asked.

"A few."

"And nobody ever asked you to prove it? With a gun?"

"No," Simon said, with a grin. "I'm very careful."

"And you only use it to impress girls?"

"Only girls," Simon said, nodding.

"And the one last year," the lawman asked. "Nell? Was she the most recent?"

Simon thought about Lisa and lied. "Yes."

"All right." Sheriff Brett stood up. "Just don't use it again! It doesn't make sense."

"Sure, yeah."

"I'll go and get your horse and bring it over here with some supplies. And then you get out of town!"

"Yeah, all right, big brother," Simon said, "whatever you say."

The sheriff nodded with some satisfaction and left the house.

***

After His brother Dan left, Simon Brett started thinking, and planning. He was still going to stop and see Lisa this afternoon at the waterhole. But it seemed to him there was only one way to get out of this mess.

He'd be safe if Clint Adams was dead.

And the only way to kill the Gunsmith was to bushwhack him. Shoot him in the back. After all, that's the way they got rid of Wild Bill Hickok.

Chapter Thirty-Four

Sheriff Brett was careful not to be seen leading Simon's horse from the livery out to his house. When he got there, Simon seemed ready to go. He had his rifle and saddlebags and was waiting in front.

"Now remember," the lawman said, "let me know where you are, and I'll tell you when to come back."

"Okay, Dan," Simon said, mounting up. "I will."

Sheriff Dan Brett watched his brother ride off . . . until he was out of sight, then turned and walked back to town.

***

As soon as Simon was sure he'd gone far enough so that he wouldn't be seen, he changed direction and headed for the waterhole. Lisa was primed and ready to give herself to him, and it was going to be her first time. That wasn't something he was about to pass up.

That is, Clint Adams wasn't going to pass it up.

***

"I thought you weren't coming," Lisa said, as Simon dismounted.

"I'm a man of my word," he replied. "I said I'd be here."

She touched the top buttons of her dress, which covered her from head-to-toe, outlining her body.

"Are we goin' in the water?" she asked.

"If that's what you want to do, Lisa," Simon said. "I told you I wouldn't force you to do anythin' you don't wanna do, remember?"

"I know," she said. "You've been a gentleman."

They started to undress.

"I'm sorry to tell you I have to leave today," he said, pulling off his boots.

"What?"

"Something's come up," he said. "I have to take care of it."

"Will you be comin' back?" she asked.

"Do you want me to come back?" he asked.

He'd almost had her the day before, in the water, but in the end she got skittish. He thought he could get her today, though, using the fact that he had to leave. Still, it had to be her decision.

When she was naked, she stood before him and said, "Then I think I'm ready."

"Are you sure?" he asked, standing and taking her by the shoulders.

"Yes, Clint," she said, "I'm ready."

He smiled and pulled her to him.

***

"You wanted to see me?" Dent asked, as he entered George's office.

"Sit, Dent."

The big man sat down.

"I heard you were seen drinkin' with Clint Adams," his boss said.

"So?" Dent said. "Who I drink with durin' my time off is my business."

"That's right," George said, "unless you happen to be talkin' about my business while you're doin' it."

"I don't talk about what goes on here, with anybody," Dent said. "I thought you knew that, boss."

"I thought I did," George said. "What were you doin' talkin' to the Gunsmith?"

"He came up to me," Dent said. "Was askin' about some stranger."

"A stranger?" George asked. "What did you tell 'im?"

"I told him we get lots of strangers here," Dent said. "I can't be expected to remember them all."

"How did he take that?"

Dent shrugged.

"He seemed fine with it," the bouncer said. "I told him to come on over and check out the girls, but he said he don't use whores."

"That's fine," George said. "We don't need him here, anyway."

"That it?" Dent asked.

"That's it," George said. "You can go back to work."

Dent left George's office, grabbed the arm of a small redhead who was walking by.

"You seen Velma?"

"Yeah," she said, "in her room, gettin' ready for work." The young girl smirked. "Takes her a little longer these days, if you know what I mean."

Dent ignored the snarky remark.

"Okay, thanks."

The girl continued down the hall, while Dent went up the stairs to talk to Velma.

Chapter Thirty-Five

After a couple of more days of asking questions, and pretty much wasting time, Clint decided to go out and see to Nell again. Maybe he could shatter that memory she had of "Clint Adams" in her mind and get a real description.

When he rode up to the house and saw Maggie and Amy's horses there, he first became angry, then just shook his head helplessly. When he knocked on the door, Noble Livingston opened it.

"You find that sonofabitch yet?" the older man demanded.

"No, not yet."

"Then what the hell are ya doin' here?"

"I need to talk to your daughter, Noble," Clint said.

"I'll send her out," the man said. "This house is too full of women."

Clint waited while Noble closed the door, and when it opened again, Nell stepped out.

"Are you mad?" she asked him.

"About what?"

"About Maggie and Amy bein' here."

"I advised them to get out of town," Clint said, "and they did. Where they went was up to them."

"My pa said you want to talk to me."

"Yes, I want to go over your description of the man again," Clint said. "But this time, Nell, I want you to close your eyes and really see him."

"What do you mean?" she asked.

"I mean see him as he really was," he said. "Get rid of any romantic notions you might still have about him. He took advantage of you, made a fool of you. Tell me what he looks like."

"I—I thought he was handsome," she said, "but I guess he wasn't. He was just sort of average, I guess."

"Tall?"

She closed her eyes. "Yes, but not as tall as you."

"And that big smile you said he had."

"It was big, but not as pleasant as I remembered," she said, her eyes still closed. It was almost like . . . like a wolf's, you know?"

"You mean," Clint said, "like a predator."

"Yes, somethin' like that," she said. "I guess—I guess he was huntin' me, wasn't he?"

"I'm afraid so."

She covered her face.

"I feel like such a fool," she said

"Well, you'll feel less like a fool the more you can tell me," Clint said.

She opened her eyes and looked at him.

"There was one thing I ignored back then, because he was so charming, but . . . he had really big ears."

***

Ansel Happ saw the rider approaching and raised his hand to stop their progress. To this point he and his family had ridden hell-bent-for-leather to get to Collinsville before Clint Adams could leave.

"Uncle Ansel," his nephew, Remy, said, reining his horse in. "The town is up ahead."

"How far?" Ansel asked.

"Half a day."

"Then we'll camp just outside the town tonight and ride in tomorrow," Ansel said.

"Why don't some of us ride in tonight, Pa?" Festus said.

"No," Ansel said, "we're stayin' together. I want Adams to see all of us comin' for him, so he knows he's gonna die."

Ansel spurred his horse on, and the rest of the Happ family followed.

***

When they were camped, Ansel set watches using every family member so that no one stood watch for more than an hour before sleeping.

But Ansel didn't take a turn. He would sleep when he wanted to, but for now he stood staring off into the distance, drinking coffee.

"Uncle," one of his nephews said, coming up next to him. "You need to sleep."

Ansel looked at the young man. He didn't know all his nephews' names, only that they were his brother's sons.

"I will," Ansel said. "I just have some thinkin' to do. You get some sleep before you go on watch."

"Yes, Uncle."

As the boy walked away, Ansel picked up the coffee pot and poured himself more coffee, then continued to look off into the distance. The lights from Collinsville were meager, so it must be a small town. Finding Clint Adams there would not be easy enough.

He was finally going to be able to avenge his son and get justice for the Happ clan.

Chapter Thirty-Six

Clint had supper alone in the small café, then left and headed for his hotel. Along the way he thought about what Nell had told him, what she remembered when her memories weren't so blocked by the romantic feelings she once had. What she said about the man's ears being big struck a chord in his memory. But he'd been talking to a lot of people, and really hadn't looked at their ears. He was going to have to start over—again!—and be more aware?

Then it hit him. He knew where he had seen an unusually large pair of ears. But he wasn't going to do anything about it tonight. It could wait until morning.

When he entered the Yellow Lady for his meeting with Dent, he saw the bouncer at a table with a beer. He went to the bar, got one for himself, and joined him.

"I was wonderin' if you forgot," Dent said.

"Not likely," Clint said. "Do you have anything for me?"

"I do," Dent said. "You know, George doesn't like me drinkin' with you."

"He said that?"

"He did," Dent said, "but I drink with who I please. I've got somethin' else for you, though. It comes from Velma."

"The tall, thin blonde?" Clint asked. "I spoke with her myself. She didn't give me anything."

"You didn't ask her the right way," Dent said.

"So what'd she tell you?"

"She remembers a stranger who came to the house one time," Dent said. "I'm guessing it was on my night off, which explains why I don't remember."

"And?"

"She described him to me," Dent said. "He kind of fits your description, but she told me something you didn't."

"His ears?"

Dent put his mug down and stared at Clint without any expression on his face. But it was in his voice when he asked, "If you already knew that—"

"I just found out today," Clint said. "Somebody told me he had large ears. And then I remembered when I saw big ears.

"The sheriff," Dent said.

"Right," Clint said, sitting back. "Do you think they're related?"

"I suppose it could be his son," Dent said, "but I never heard that Sheriff Brett had any kids. What about a brother? A younger brother."

"Could be," Clint said. "I'm going to ask him."

"Tonight?"

"No, I'll wait til morning," Clint said. "Thanks for your help, Dent."

"Don't thank me," Dent said. "I told you, anybody George Callaghan hates is a friend of mine . . . almost."

"If you don't like him, why work for him?"

"I told you," Dent said. "He pays me well."

"I don't think I'd work for a man I hate no matter how much he paid me," Clint commented.

"Well," Dent said, "I ain't the Gunsmith. You can pretty much do what you like."

"I don't know about that," Clint said, "but thanks for the information, Dent."

"If I was you, I wouldn't try comin' around the whorehouse," Dent warned. "Callaghan might set me against you. I wouldn't look forward to that."

"Neither would I, Dent," Clint said, and left the saloon.

***

Walking back to his hotel, Clint gave some thought to what he'd found out. If the sheriff was related to the imposter, then he knew his real name and where he was. Clint didn't like the idea of going up against a badge. But this had nothing to do with Brett being the law. And if he was a man trying to protect his family, there was no way Clint could really hold that against him. But the imposter had to be stopped from using Clint's name. If he wanted to continue taking advantage of gullible young women, he was going to have to do it under his own name.

It was ironic. Clint still had the spectre of the Happ family hanging over him, intending to avenge their dead relative. And now, here in Collinsville, he once again might have found a situation where he was going up against family members. He didn't have family of his own but understood being forced into a showdown out of loyalty and commitment. Men shouldn't have to pay for that with their lives. If and when the Happ family caught up to him, he hoped he would be able to convince them of that. If he wasn't, there was going to be a lot of gunplay.

When he got to his room, he hung his gunbelt on the bedpost, made sure his window was locked, and jammed the back of a wooden chair underneath the doorknob.

Just to be on the safe side.

Chapter Thirty-Seven

Sheriff Dan Brett was on the street the next morning when the eleven strangers came riding down the street. It was odd for that many men to come to Collinsville at the same time, unless they were headed for the whorehouse, or looking for somebody.

Brett stepped into the street so the riders wouldn't be able to go by without seeing him. The man in front spotted him and halted their progress.

"'mornin', Sheriff," he said.

"'mornin'," the sheriff said. "What brings all you fellas to our little town?"

"We heard you got a good whorehouse here," the head man said. "That true?"

"It's about the only thing we got that's worth anythin'," Brett said. "All the way at the end of the street. You can't miss it."

"Thank you, kindly."

Brett stepped back onto the boardwalk as the eleven riders continued on.

***

When they reached the whorehouse, Ansel turned, said, "Wait here," and dismounted.

"How come he gets to go in and see the whores?" one of the cousins asked.

"Because he's pa," Festus said.

Ansel knocked on the door and waited. It was opened by Velma, the tall, faded blonde.

"Damn," she said, looking behind him, "folks are knockin' on our door early, these days. Can ya come back for a poke when we're open?"

"We ain't here for no poke," Ansel said. "I'm here to see a fella named Callaghan."

"That's the boss," Velma said. "I'll tell 'im yer here. You got a name?"

"Happ, Ansel Happ."

"Just a minute."

Velma closed the door. Ansel waited patiently until she opened it again.

"Follow me," she said.

***

"Who're all those men out front?" Dent asked Velma.

"I don't know, but some feller named Happ wanted to see George," she answered, "and they ain't here for the girls."

As Velma went back to the front, Dent moved down the hall and stood near George's door to hopefully catch some of the conversation that was about to take place.

***

Velma led Ansel down a hall to George Callaghan's office.

"Go ahead in," she said.

Ansel opened the door and entered. A man stood up from his desk and walked around with his hand out.

"Mr. Happ? Glad to meet you. I'm George Callaghan."

Ansel shook the man's hand.

"You're the one sent me the telegram about Adams," Happ said. "Is he still here?"

"He is, over at the hotel," George told him.

"We ran into the sheriff on the way in here," Ansel said. "Is he gonna be a problem?"

"I doubt it," George said. "He's got his own troubles to take care of. I think he might be very happy if you and your family take care of the Gunsmith. And when you're done, why don't you all come back here?"

"I don't use no diseased whores," Ansel said, "but I'm sure my brothers and nephews will be back."

"Not your sons?"

"I'd just as soon cut their dicks off," Ansel said. He turned to leave, then stopped. "Tell me somethin'."

"Anything," George said.

"How'd you know we was lookin' for Adams?" Ansel asked. "And why would you send me that telegram?"

"I've got contacts all over the country," George said. "When Adams rode in, I knew somebody out there must be lookin' for him. When I heard your name and where you were from, I figured what the hell?"

"But why do you care if I find Adams or not?"

"This is a small town," George said, "but it's got potential, and I'm here on the ground floor. Men like Adams are a thing of the past. We don't need him around here."

Ansel nodded and left.

When he was gone, George went back to his desk and sat. Clint Adams getting killed by the Happ family in Collinsville was sure to put the town on the map. Everybody knew that Hickok was killed in Deadwood, and that the Earps got shot up in Tombstone. When word got out about the Gunsmith being killed in Collinsville, George was going to have to hire a lot more girls to handle the crowds. Maybe even open a bigger place. All he had to do now was sit back and wait.

Chapter Thirty-Eight

Dent went out the back door while Ansel Happ went out the front and mounted his horse.

"What'd you get, Pa?" Festus asked.

"Adams is at the hotel."

"We gonna go get 'im?" Festus asked.

"Word's gonna get around that we're in town," Ansel said. "Let's get something to eat and let Adams think about it for a while."

"But what if he leaves town?" Festus asked.

"He's the goddamned Gunsmith," Ansel said. "He ain't about to run."

"So where we goin'?"

"We passed a café as we rode in," Ansel said. "Let's go back there. Once our bellies are full, we'll be ready for Clint Adams."

They all turned and rode back toward the center of town.

***

Clint was in the lobby of the hotel when he heard the riders outside. He went to the door and saw Sheriff Brett talking to the leader of the eleven men. It wasn't a stretch to figure this was the Happ family. After talking briefly with the sheriff, the riders continued on. If they weren't the Happs, then they were riders from some ranch headed for the whorehouse.

Clint's intention had been to go to the café for breakfast and then talk to the sheriff. Once those eleven riders had vacated the street, he stepped outside and started walking to the café.

***

Clint was eating his breakfast when Dent walked in.

"The desk clerk at the hotel told me where you'd be," Dent said, sitting across from Clint.

"You want some coffee?" Clint asked.

"You know a fella named Ansel Happ?"

"I know a clan named Happ," Clint said.

"So you know they're lookin' for you?"

"I figured," Clint said. "Didn't know for sure."

"Well, you do now," Dent said. "Seems my boss sent them a telegram, told 'em you were here."

"I saw those riders earlier this morning," Clint said. "Eleven of them?"

"That's what it looked like to me."

"Well, thanks for the warning, Dent."

"I ain't just warnin' you," Dent said. "I'm offering to help."

"You'd stand with me against eleven men? Why?"

Dent shrugged.

"Bein' a bouncer gets kinda borin' after a while," he said. "And like I said before, I don't like my boss, and now I don't like what he did, settin' you up for these men."

"You interested in what their beef with me is?"

"Doesn't matter to me what the beef is," Dent said, "eleven against one don't sit right with me."

"I tell you what," Clint said. "Don't be seen with me but keep your eyes open. If push comes to shove, I could use an extra gun, but I'd just as soon they don't know I've got one."

"I get it," Dent said. He headed for the door but stopped there and turned back. "Riders comin'."

"Okay," Clint said, "get out of here but stay close."

"Right."

Dent wasn't the only one to leave. A couple of other tables of diners smelled trouble, dropped money onto the table and scurried out.

"Is there gonna be trouble?" the waiter asked Clint.

"Not if I can help it," Clint said. "You just do your job and you'll be fine."

"Yessir."

The waiter was in the kitchen when the eleven riders dismounted and crowded into the small café. Clint, seated in the back, watched and listened as he continued to eat.

***

As they entered, the lead man directed the others as to where to sit, so that he ended up at a table with just one other man.

Clint noticed that about half the men wore sidearms, while the others carried either a rifle or a shotgun.

"Waiter!" he shouted.

The waiter came out of the kitchen and nervously looked at all the men who had just entered. Then he looked over at Clint.

"Yes, sir?" he said to the leader.

"Bring us all bacon-and-eggs," the man said. "And coffee."

"Yessir."

About half a dozen of the riders—all dust covered and grimy from the trail—were seated very close to Clint. The man he saw as the leader was across the room with one other man, but he could hear the conversation.

"Pa," the other man said, "when do we go get Adams?"

"Shut up, Festus," the leader said. "Don't talk about that here. We go when I say so."

Pretty soon nobody was talking. All the men ate and drank coffee voraciously, noisily, and with no manners. Other diners quickly finished their food and left, so that only the eleven riders and Clint were left in the café.

That gave Clint an idea.

Chapter Thirty-Nine

Clint finished his breakfast quietly while the others paid him no mind and ate like wolves. The waiter remained in the kitchen but stuck his head out from time to time.

When Clint finished, he dropped some money onto the table, then stood, picked up his hat, and walked over to the table where the leader of the riders was eating. When he stopped by the table the man looked up at him.

"You want somethin'?" he demanded.

"You must be the head of the Happ family," Clint said. "That right?"

The man dropped his fork and sat back.

"I'm Ansel Happ. You're Adams?"

"That's right."

The rest of the family, hearing this, dropped their utensils and reached for their guns.

"Stop!" Ansel shouted.

"Tell them to keep eating," Clint said. "We're just going to talk. This place is too small for any kind of a shootout. A lot of your family will end up killing each other."

"You got that right," Ansel said. "Everyone, keep eating until I say different!"

Slowly, they all picked up their forks, and eventually started eating.

"Do you wanna sit?" Ansel said. "Festus can move."

"No, I'm fine standing," Clint said. "I want you to know your son, Uriah, called the play back in Big Fork. He pushed too hard and didn't leave me a choice."

"I know that," Ansel said. "He was always a little fool."

"Then why all this?" Clint asked, waving his left arm. He kept his right hand hanging down by his gun.

"Because he was my son," Ansel said. "Fool or not, his death has to be avenged."

"At what cost?" Clint asked. "More family members will die. I have no desire to kill any more of them."

"They all know the risk," Ansel said. "I haven't ordered any of them to be here. They all had a choice. It's called family loyalty."

Clint looked around the room. The family members were eating but keeping their eyes on him and their patriarch.

"I don't have a family," Clint said, aloud. "Is that kind of loyalty something to die for?"

"We know who you are, Adams," Ansel said, "and what you do. How many of us do you think you can kill?"

"Mr. Happ," Clint said, "that would depend on how quickly I can reload."

Clint turned and walked out, hoping he had given the family something to think about.

***

"Pa," Festus said, as Clint left, "he don't seem scared at all."

"Do you think he woulda lived this long if he scared easy, boy?" Ansel asked.

"But what if he—"

"Finish your breakfast, boy," Ansel said. "We got killin' to do, after this."

***

From the café, Clint went directly to the sheriff's office.

"I've been expectin' you," Brett said, as he walked in.

"I saw you talking to those men who rode in," Clint said. "Do you know why they're here?"

"They asked for the whorehouse."

"I doubt they were looking for whores," Clint said. "Seems George Callaghan sent a telegram that brought them here."

"For you?"

Clint nodded.

"They're the Happ family," he said. "I had a run in with one of them in Big Fork. They're looking for revenge."

"You gonna leave town?"

"Run?" Clint asked. "I can't do that. Once I run, I'll be running forever."

"And how different is that from what you do now?" the lawman asked.

"Big difference," Clint said, "and I don't have time to explain it to you. We have other business."

"What's that?"

"The man I'm looking for is related to you. How? Son? Brother?"

Brett stared for a few moments, and Clint wondered if the next words out of his mouth would be the truth, or a lie?

"Brother," he finally said. "I didn't even know he existed until he came here last year and introduced himself. Seems after my father died my mother grieved for years before marrying again. He's at least twenty years younger than I am."

"Why is he impersonating me?" Clint asked. "Doesn't he know that can get him killed?"

"I've told him that," Brett said. "He only does it with women. Look, he's an idiot, Adams, but he ain't hurtin' anybody."

"Tell that to Nell Livingston and her family. Tell that to Noble."

"Noble's a hothead," Brett said. "I can cool him off. You're the one I'm afraid of. I just found my brother, Adams. I can't have you kill 'im."

"What makes you think I want to kill him?" Clint asked. "I just want him to stop impersonating me. What would happen if the Happ family rode in looking for the Gunsmith, and found him, instead?"

"The kid's actually pretty good with a gun," Brett said, "but he couldn't stand against that many."

"How good?" Clint asked.

"What?"

"How good is he?"

"Not as good as you, but I'd put him up against a lot of so-called gunfighters. Why?"

"I've got an idea," Clint proposed, "but I'll need your help."

Chapter Forty

"Do you know where he is?" Clint asked, after outlining his idea to the lawman.

"He sent me a message."

"Can you send him one?"

"Sure."

"Then do it," Clint said. "Maybe we can teach him a lesson and put him to good use at the same time."

"If he lives through it."

"Right," Clint said, "if he lives. Either way, I want to see him."

"Not to kill 'im?"

"No," Clint said, "not to kill 'im."

Brett gave it some thought, then nodded and said, "I'll send a message."

"Okay," Clint said, "now I just need a way to hold off the Happs."

"Are they law-abidin'?" Brett asked.

"I don't actually know," Clint admitted. "I haven't heard anything about any of them being wanted. Why?"

Brett grinned.

"Now I have an idea."

***

Before the Happ clan finished their breakfast, Sheriff Brett appeared at the door of the café.

"Sheriff," Ansel said, "what can we do for you?"

"Well, when you and your family are done here, you can leave your guns behind."

"What?"

"We have a law here," the sheriff said. "No guns inside the town limits."

"We need our guns," Festus said.

"Not in town you don't," Brett said.

"Is that a real law?" Ansel asked.

"That depends."

"On what?"

"Are you law-abidin' people?" Brett asked. "If not, then I guess it won't matter if it's a real law or not."

"We ain't outlaws," Ansel said. "We don't break the law."

"Then it's a real law," Brett said. "I'll take your guns to my office, you can have them back when you leave town."

"We just saw a man leave here wearin' a gun," Ansel said.

"Is that right? I'll have to find 'im and take it away."

"He's the Gun—" Festus started, but Ansel kicked him under the table.

"I'd like to see that," Ansel said. "You boys heard the sheriff. Leave your guns on the tables when you're finished eatin'."

They all grumbled but nodded.

"I appreciate that, Mr. Happ," the sheriff said.

Brett left the café before Ansel could ask him how he knew their name.

***

The sheriff met Clint in an alley down the street from the café.

"How'd it go?"

"They're gonna leave their guns," Brett said. "I'll be takin' them over to my office."

"That's good."

"Yeah, it is," Brett said, "as long as you stay in town. Once you ride out, it's open season."

"Sheriff," Clint said, "it's always open season on me."

Chapter Forty-One

As they left their guns on their tables and readied to leave the café Festus asked, "Pa, how the hell we gonna go up against Adams without guns?"

"Don't worry, boy," Ansel said, "he ain't goin' nowhere."

As they left the café, they passed the sheriff waiting outside.

"Enjoy your stay," Brett said.

"You just be ready to return them guns, Sheriff," Ansel told him.

Brett went inside to collect the hardware.

***

"How did you get them to give up their guns?" Dent asked. He was waiting for Clint in the lobby of his hotel.

"That was the sheriff's idea," Clint said, "and it was a good one."

"But eventually he's gonna have to give them back," Dent pointed out.

"Yeah, but hopefully," Clint said, "we'll control when that time will be."

"We?"

"You did offer to help, right?"

"Uh, yeah, right. What's the next step?"

"The sheriff's brother."

"So they *are* related," Dent said. "Big ears and all."

"The sheriff says this Simon Brett came to town last year, introduced himself as the sheriff's half-brother."

"And he believed him?"

"He says Simon had proof," Clint said. "So, yeah, he believes him."

"All right," Dent said. "Is he gonna help you find 'im?"

"He is."

"And then you're gonna . . . what? Not kill 'im, right?"

"Right," Clint said. "I'm going to make him do penance."

"Penance?"

"He's going to pay for impersonating me," Clint said, "by helping me—us—stand against them."

"And why do you think he's gonna do that?" Dent asked.

"Well, for one thing," Clint said, "the sheriff's going to tell him to. And second, he'll have to deal with me if he doesn't agree."

"Not much of a choice," Dent said. "Hear it from his brother, or from you."

"Right."

"So that's why you had their guns taken away," Dent said. "They can't do a thing to you without them."

"While we're all in town," Clint added. "Once we leave town, all bets are off."

"So you're gonna stay in town until the sheriff gets his brother back here?"

"Right," Clint said. "I'm going to use the sheriff's brother to help fight off the Happ family, thereby killing two birds with one stone."

"Hey, that's pretty clever," Dent said. "Did you make that up?"

"No, it's pretty ancient," Clint said. "Look, when I need you, where will you be?"

"Either the whorehouse, the Yellow Lady, or the Last Bullet," Dent said.

"Good," Clint thought. "Now all he needs to do is stay alive til the sheriff's brother gets here."

"You think they'll try to kill you without guns?" Dent asked.

"Some of them might," Clint said. "Their leader, Ansel, may try to keep them all in line, but some of them are young and they've all got this thing about family honor."

"Then why don't you grab Ansel?" Dent asked.

"Grab him?"

"Snatch 'im," Dent said, "and hold him somewhere. That way if any of them come for you, you can bargain with them."

"Where would I keep him?" Clint asked.

"I think I might have an idea about that," Dent said.

***

"What are we supposed to do without our guns?" Festus asked his father, outside the café, after the sheriff had walked off, juggling their iron.

"Keep yourselves occupied," Ansel said, "but ready and out of trouble. And Festus . . ."

"Yeah, Pa?"

"Keep your hotheaded cousins in line."

"Sure, Pa," Festus said, as an idea came into his head, "sure."

Chapter Forty-Two

Festus looked across the table at his cousins, Hector's son Ezekial and Levon's son, Travis.

"We're gonna get 'im ourselves," he said.

"But, what about what your pa said?" Zeke asked.

"And our pas are goin' along with him," Travis pointed out.

"That's because they're old," Festus said. "Uriah was one of us, my brother, your cousin," Festus said. "And Adams killed him. So we're gonna kill Adams."

"With no guns?" Zeke asked.

"We could get guns," Festus said, "but I have a better idea."

"Like what?" Travis asked.

"You boys still have your knives, right?"

***

The first thing Clint noticed when he entered the sheriff's office was all the guns piled on top of his desk.

"Are you going to lock those up?" Clint asked.

"I was just about to move them to a cell," Brett said. "You wanna help me carry 'em?"

"Sure."

They gathered up the guns, carried them into the cell block, set them on a cot in a cell, and then Brett locked the door.

They went back to Brett's desk and sat on either side of it.

"What about your brother?" Clint asked.

"I sent him a message," Brett replied. "I told him the coast is clear to come back."

"How long will it take?"

"If he starts back as soon as he gets it, he should be here tonight."

Clint decided not to tell the lawman the idea he and Dent had to get more time.

"Okay," he said, instead, "let me know when he gets here, and we'll talk to him together."

"I appreciate that," Brett said. "Maybe you can straighten him out."

"I'll likely either be at my hotel or the Yellow Lady."

"I'll let you know as soon as he gets here," Brett said. "Meanwhile, try not to kill anybody, or get killed between now and then."

"I'll do my best."

***

Dent was in the hotel lobby when Clint got there.

"Where is he?" Clint asked.

"Looks like he's settin' himself up at the Yellow Lady."

"Any family with him?"

"No, he's alone," Dent said. "The others have scattered, some at Declan's, some are even at Lady George's."

"Is Callaghan wondering where you are?"

"I told him I was takin' the day off, but I'd be back tonight."

"Okay, then," Clint said. "If he's alone, let's grab him."

"You talk to Sheriff Brett?"

"Yeah, but I didn't tell him what we're planning. We're going to be dealing with his brother when he gets here. I don't want to give him too much to think about."

"Well, he's done his part by takin' all their guns," Dent pointed out.

"Yes, he did," Clint said. "I appreciate it, and I'll appreciate what you're going to do."

"Hey," Dent said, "it's real easy to get bored in this town."

"Let's see what we can do about that," Clint said.

***

Ansel Happ looked up from his drink as a man came through the batwing doors of the Yellow Lady Saloon and approached his table.

"Can I do somethin' for ya?" he asked.

"No," Dent said, "but I think I might be able to do somethin' for you."

"Like what?"

"I heard that you're here for the Gunsmith," Dent said.

"That's right."

"But your guns were taken away."

"That's also right."

"Well," Dent said, "I think I can get them back for you."

"How?"

"If you come with me," Dent said, "I'll show you."

Ansel looked Dent up and down.

"How come you still got your gun?" he asked. "If there's a law against guns in the town limit?"

"Because there is no such law, Mr. Happ," Dent said.

"And why do you wanna help me?"

"My boss doesn't like the Gunsmith," Dent said. "He wants him gone, one way or another. Even your way."

Chapter Forty-Three

Clint was walking from his hotel to the Yellow Lady when they came at him from an alley. There were several people on the street, both on his side and across from him, but, when they saw what was happening, they scattered and ran for cover.

The three men surrounded him, knives in their hands.

"You're gonna pay for killin' my brother," one of them said. Clint recognized him as the man who had been sitting with Ansel Happ. That made him Ansel's son, and Uriah's brother. The other two were either brothers or cousins.

"Now, just relax, boys," Clint said.

"Festus," one of the other men said, "he still got his gun. How come?"

Festus looked and frowned. It was as if he was so intent on cutting Clint that he didn't notice the gun until it was pointed out to him.

"Yeah," the other one said, "how come?"

"You ain't supposed to have a gun," Festus said to Clint.

"Well, I'm not about to walk these streets unarmed with you and your family in town. Look what can happen." He indicated their knives.

"Festus . . ." one of the others said.

"He won't shoot us," Festus said. "Not while we only have knives."

"Think again, Festus," Clint said. "I'm not about to let you idiots stick me. I'll shoot you, first—maybe in the knee, maybe between the eyes."

Now the three of them were starting to have second thoughts.

"I'll bet your father doesn't know you're here, does he?" Clint asked.

Festus looked nervous.

"I tell you what," Clint said. "I'm willing to let you boys back off. Go ahead, step back, that's it . . . and now, get out of here! Before I change my mind."

The two men Clint assumed were cousins were the first to turn and run. Festus stared at him, firmed his jaw, then turned and walked away.

Clint, happy he hadn't had to shoot the three men, turned and headed for the Yellow Lady.

***

When Dent didn't appear at the Yellow Lady, Clint started to worry. The plan had been for the bouncer to grab Ansel and stick him somewhere, then come and meet in the saloon. But perhaps Dent, a bouncer, didn't have what it took to get the jump on Ansel Happ.

Clint left the Yellow Lady and headed for the Last Bullet. Hopefully, he'd hear from the sheriff about his brother.

***

When the office door opened, Sheriff Brett expected his brother, Simon. Instead, he was looking at Ansel Happ, who was pointing a gun at him.

"What the hell—" he said.

"Change of plans," Ansel said. "We've come for our guns."

Five more men filed in behind him.

"Where'd you get that gun?" Brett asked.

"It belonged to a man named Dent," Ansel said. "He had an idea of takin' me somewhere and holdin' me there, but he wasn't man enough."

"And where is he now?"

Ansel smiled.

"He got too close to me," he said. "Luckily, he was plannin' on holdin' me in the whorehouse, and some of

186

my family were already there." He indicated the man with him. "Where are our guns?"

"I'm not gonna tell you."

Ansel looked at his family members.

"Hector," he said, to his brother, "find the keys and check the cells."

"Right."

The keys were hanging on the wall, so Hector grabbed them and went into the cell block.

"Guns!" he shouted.

"Go get 'em," Ansel said to the others. "And then we'll go and find the rest of the boys."

"You're not gonna get away with this," Sheriff Brett warned.

"I've discovered this town doesn't have real law," Ansel said, "so I think we will."

When his brother came out with his nephews, Hector said, "What about him?" indicating the sheriff. "Kill 'im?"

"He may not be much of one, but he is the sheriff here," Ansel said. "Lock him in a cell. When we're done here, somebody will find him, and we'll be long gone."

"After killin' Clint Adams?" Hector said.

"Right," Ansel said, "after killin' Clint Adams."

Chapter Forty-Four

When Dent didn't show up at the Last Bullet Clint knew something had gone wrong.

"'nother beer?" Bub asked.

"I don't think so," Clint said. "Listen, you know what goes on in this town. You got any idea what the Happs have been doing since they got here?"

"Drinkin' at Declan's, fuckin' at Lady George's—"

"That must be it," Clint said, more to himself than Bub. Dent was going to take Ansel to the whorehouse and stick him in a room. He must've run into other members of the family.

"Thanks, Bub." He turned to leave.

"What do I tell Dent if he shows up?" the bartender asked.

"I don't think he will," Clint said.

***

This was one time when Clint didn't have to knock on the door of Lady George's in order to get in.

It was whorehouse business hours.

He went inside, found the girls sitting alone looking upset.

"We're closed," Velma approached him and said.

"Why?" Clint asked. "Where is everybody?"

"We sent all the men home."

"Where's Dent?" Clint asked. "Is he here?"

"Dent's dead," a man's voice said.

He turned and saw George Callaghan.

"What? How? Who did it?"

"You tell me," George said. "Apparently he was doin' somethin' for you. He brought a fella here, and that fella and some other customers killed him. Turns out they were all part of the same family."

"The Happs."

"What the hell is goin' on, Adams?"

"I'm going to find out," Clint said. He turned and left.

***

When he entered the sheriff's office it was empty.

"Sheriff?"

"Back here!"

He went to the cell block, found the lawman locked in a cell.

"Don't tell me, let me guess," Clint said. "Ansel Happ?"

"And some of his family," Brett said. "They got all their guns."

"And now they're out looking for me?"

"I think he's looking for the rest of his family," Brett said.

"Where are the keys?" Clint asked.

"Somewhere in the office."

Clint didn't find them on the wall peg where they usually were, but on the floor in a corner, where they had been tossed. He released the sheriff.

"How many of them were there?" he asked.

"Six."

"So they're looking for the other five. If I can find them in smaller groups, I might be able to take care of them."

"You'll need help," Sheriff Brett said.

"Are you any good with a gun?" Clint asked.

"Not really," Brett said.

At that moment the door opened, and a young man came bursting in.

"But he is," Brett said. "Clint Adams, meet my brother, Simon."

The young man with large ears stared at Clint, swallowed, and then turned to run.

"Stop, Simon!"

"You sent me a message that he was gone!" Simon said. "What is this, Dan?"

"Mr. Adams needs our help, Simon," Brett said, "and then he'll forget about you using his name."

Simon looked at Clint again.

"That is," Clint said, "if you promise never to do it again."

"I—I swear," Simon said. "Never again."

"Your brother says you're good with a gun," Clint said.

"P-pretty good."

"There are eleven men who have come to town to kill me," Clint said. "I had the help of a man named Dent, but it looks like they killed him already."

"Eleven?" Simon asked. "Against two of us?"

"Three," the lawman said.

"You ain't good with a gun, Dan," Simon said.

The sheriff walked to a gun rack on the wall and took down a shotgun.

"With this scatter gun," he said, "I don't have to be good. I can't miss."

Okay, then," Clint said. "Grab a rifle, kid, and we'll be set."

Chapter Forty-Five

It took Sheriff Brett a few more moments to convince Simon that Clint didn't want to kill him.

"I told him you're good enough with a gun to help him," the lawman said. "Lucky for you, he needs help."

"We still have some daylight," Clint said.

"Wouldn't darkness help?" Sheriff Brett asked. "They don't know the layout of the town."

"I don't know it so well, either, except for saloons," Clint said.

"Well, I know every inch of it," Brett said.

Clint looked out the window.

"I'd have to lay low for a couple of more hours," Clint said. "Hiding doesn't suit me. And besides, by then the whole family will be back together again. I'd like to find them while they're still split up."

"So we won't be facing eleven at one time?" Simon asked. "I'm in favor of that."

"Okay then," Sheriff Brett said, "where to first?"

"I was told they were drinking in both Declan's and the Yellow Lady. Let's try them."

***

They stopped outside the Yellow Lady and looked through the window.

"There's three of them in here," Clint said.

"Let's get 'em," Simon said.

"Easy," Clint said. "I can handle them, but I'd just as soon not kill any."

"Really?" Simon asked. "I thought that was what you did."

"We'll talk after," Clint said. "Right now, you stay here unless I call you."

"I'll go around back," Brett said. "If we can take them alive, I'll put them in a cell."

"Okay," Clint said. "I'll give you thirty seconds to get around there."

"Should be easy," Brett said. "This alley—"

"Go!"

Brett slipped into the darkness of the alley.

"Remember," Clint said to Simon, "not til I call you."

"I got it."

Clint went through the door, fully aware that he was being backed by two men he didn't know a thing about. What would they do in a crisis? He might have to find out the hard way.

There were other customers in the Yellow Lady, but only those three reacted when Clint walked in. They were armed, so apparently Ansel had found them after reclaiming the weapons from the sheriff's office. Why he left them in this saloon was anybody's guess.

They all started to get to their feet as Clint walked in.

"Take it easy!" he shouted. "Let's not make this messy."

The three men froze. One was older than the other two.

"I'm guessing you're Ansel's brother," he said, pointing.

"That's right," the man said. "I'm Levon."

"Levon, I need to take you and these boys—"

"These are my sons."

"Okay, good, I need to take you and your sons over to the jail."

"We ain't done nothin'," Levon said.

"I know," Clint said, "I just need to lock you up before you do something."

While he talked, Clint scanned the interior. There was a second floor, a doorway in the back, and one behind the bar. He assumed the sheriff would be coming in the back, so he kept a wary eye on the other doorway. He still didn't like that Ansel had given these men back their guns but left them there.

Why weren't they all together?

***

The sheriff found his way to the back, went through the unlocked door, into a storeroom. There was nothing there but supplies, so he made his way to the door he heard voices emanating from. Gun in hand, he stood there and peered out.

***

It occurred to Simon, as he waited outside, that he had a way out of this mess. If it came to shooting in the saloon, and Adams called for him, all he had to do was stay where he was. If the Gunsmith got himself killed, Simon wouldn't have to worry about whether or not Adams was telling the truth and didn't plan to kill him.

But as he stared through the window, it looked to him like the three men, who were half in, half out of their chairs, were scared. Would they draw on the Gunsmith and go three against one? And if they did, according to Adams' reputation, he could handle three men with no trouble.

If Simon left Adams hanging, and the Gunsmith killed those three, he was sure to come after Simon, next.

So he palmed his iron and waited to see if Clint Adams would deal him into the play.

Chapter Forty-Six

Something was wrong.

Finding these three here, separated from the others, was the kind of thing he had hoped for, but they had their guns. That meant Ansel had found them, and armed them, but why leave them here? The only way to face somebody like the Gunsmith was together.

Clint's eyes flicked up to the second floor, where there was a railing overlooking the first floor.

Shit.

This was a trap set for him, and he had walked right into it.

He noticed Levon's eyes also flicking toward the bar, and the second level. His sons were biting their lips, waiting for a command.

"This is a bad idea, Levon," Clint said. "No matter who else is here, you and your boys get it first."

If he could dispatch these three quickly, that'd leave eight and, hopefully, he had two guns backing him up. That was a hell of a lot better than the eleven-to-one odds he had started with.

But if this was a trap . . .

And at that moment, he found out it was.

Suddenly, men came pouring out of the doorway behind the bar and appeared on the upper floor. Clint had to act fast, he had no choice. He drew his gun and quickly shot Levon and his two sons, leaving them draped over their table.

Ansel and the rest of his family began to fire, and Clint knew Simon wouldn't hear him as he yelled, "Simon! Now!" He just hoped the young man read the situation and came in with his gun blazing.

Sheriff Brett came out the back door and the room exploded with the sound of his shotgun as he let go with both barrels.

But all of the Happ family's attention was on Clint. Hot lead began flying at him from all directions. Clint quickly overturned a table and got behind it. Bullets chewed at it, and some even worked their way through. A single slug creased his shoulder as he reloaded quickly.

Simon Brett came through the door, gun in hand, and started firing. Sheriff Brett, having fired both barrels of his shotgun, tossed it aside, drew his gun and started pulling the trigger.

The bartender, crouched down behind the bar, stood up and shouted, "Adams!" When Clint looked over the man tossed him an over-and-under shotgun. Clint caught it in both hands, turned, fired one barrel, then the other.

Broken, bloodied bodies began to cover the floor. When it got quiet, Clint could hear the sound of guns being reloaded, including his.

"Are we going to reload and keep this up, Ansel?" he shouted from behind the chewed-up table. "How many more family members do you want to lose?"

"It don't matter," Ansel shouted, also crouched behind an overturned table. "My boys are dead. I can't go home and tell their Mama they're dead. I'd rather be dead myself."

To make his point he stood up, gun in hand, and looked around.

Clint stood from behind his table and faced him.

"You sonofa—" Ansel started, intending to shoot, but Clint fired first. The bullet struck Ansel in the chest and knocked him onto his back.

Clint looked around at the remaining members of the Happ family. Four of the eleven seemed to still be standing. He, the sheriff, and Simon all turned to face them.

"Is this over?" Clint asked. "Or do you all want to die?"

Hector, the last of the older Happs—now the patriarch, with Ansel being dead—said, "It's over." He dropped his gun, and so did the other, younger Happ men.

Clint looked at Dan and Simon Brett.

"Are you all right?" he asked the lawman.

"Pretty much," the sheriff said. "They seemed to all he shootin' at you."

Clint looked down at the table he was crouching behind. It wouldn't be used again as anything but kindling.

Clint turned and looked at Simon, who was staring around at the carnage with wide eyes.

"Are you hit, Simon?" Clint asked.

Simon looked down at himself and said, "I don't think so." Then he looked at Clint. "But you are."

Clint looked at his bloody shoulder, then probed it with his hand.

"It's not bad," he said.

"All right, you fellas march over to the jail with me," Sheriff Brett said to Hector and his boys.

"If you don't need me," Simon said to Clint, "I'll help my brother get this cleaned up."

"I don't need you tonight," Clint said, "but I will tomorrow."

"For what?" Simon asked.

"You're going to visit your son," Clint said. "And there are some people you're going to have to do some apologizing to."

"I guess you're right," Simon said. "Startin' with you, I guess."

"You did your apologizing to me when you stepped up here," Clint said. "But after seeing this, I don't think you'll want to go around telling people you're me, anymore."

Simon looked down at the bloodied bodies on the floor and said, "I guess you're right about that, too, Mr. Adams."

Coming October 27, 2020

THE GUNSMITH
464
The Ticket Clerk

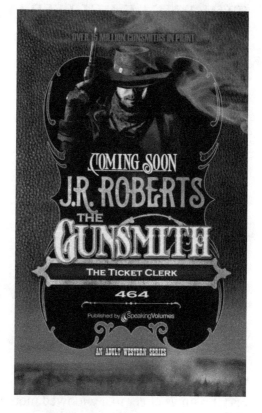

For more information
visit: www.SpeakingVolumes.us

Coming November 27, 2020

A Special Christmas Edition

THE GUNSMITH GIANT
THE JINGLE BELL TRAIL

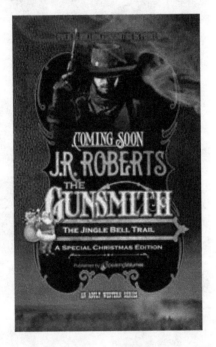

Clint Adams follows the jingle bell trail to a town where he brings Christmas cheer to a widowed mother and her little boy.

For more information
visit: www.SpeakingVolumes.us

On Sale Now!

THE GUNSMITH
462
The Gypsy King

**For more information
visit:** www.SpeakingVolumes.us

On Sale Now!

THE GUNSMITH *series*
Books 430 - 461

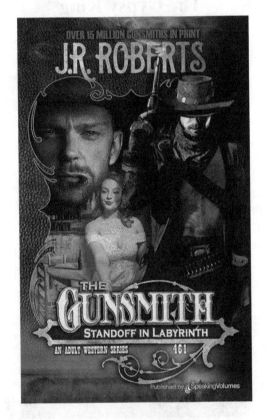

For more information
visit: www.SpeakingVolumes.us

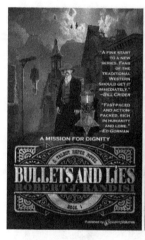

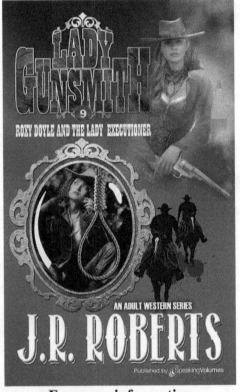

On Sale!

**Award-Winning Author
Robert J. Randisi (J.R. Roberts)**

**For more information
visit:** www.SpeakingVolumes.us

CPSIA information can be obtained
at www.ICGtesting.com
Printed in the USA
LVHW031729180521
687788LV00005B/268